A Dream to Cherish

A Dream to Cherish

Angela Elwell Hunt

Tyndale House Publishers, Inc.
Wheaton, Illinois

In loving memory of Glenn Phillips

This book could not have been written without Terry Plecas, skating coach at Southland Skating in Pinellas Park, Florida; Dr. Ronnie Massey of the Pinellas County Health Department; and my editors, LaVonne Neff—who almost believes Cassie and Max live with me—and the wonderfully efficient Karen Ball.

Thank you, ladies, for your time and help.

Library of Congress Cataloging-in-Publication Data

Hunt, Angela Elwell, date
  A dream to cherish / Angela Elwell Hunt.
    p.   cm. — (Cassie Perkins ; #4)
  Summary: Fourteen-year-old Cassie's adjustment to a new school and a new stepfather and stepbrother is eased by friendship with the dazzling championship roller skater Arien, with whom Cassie shares her faith in God when a shocking surprise changes their lives.
  ISBN 0-8423-1064-9
  [1. Christian life—Fiction.   2. AIDS (Disease)—Fiction.
3. Stepfamilies—Fiction.   4. Roller skating—Fiction.   5. Schools—Fiction.]   I. Title.   II. Series: Hunt, Angela Elwell, date
Cassie Perkins ; #4.
PZ7.H9115Caw   1992
[Fic]—dc20   91-32996

Printed in the United States of America

99 98 97 96 95 94 93 92
8   7   6   5   4   3   2   1

Important People in My Life, by Cassie Perkins

1. Glen Perkins, my dad. ♥♥♥♥♥
   A systems analyst at Kennedy Space Center, and my favorite singer. Handsome, even if balding. Now divorced from my mom and living in a condo. Sometimes I wonder if he gets lonely, but his work seems to keep him busy.

2. Claire Louise Perkins Harris, my mom. ♥♥♥♥♥
   An interior decorator. Now married to Tom Harris, a lawyer. Still has stars in her eyes.

3. Max Brian Perkins, my brother. ♥♥♥♥♥!
   Max lives with Dad in the condo. Max is the only ten-year-old in the ninth grade at my school. He's a genius, and he has epilepsy, which scares me to death, but Max deals with it. He says a lot of geniuses have had epilepsy.

4. Dribbles, my Chinese Pug. ♥♥♥♥
   She's just a puppy. Tom got her for me the day my old dog, Suki, died.

5. Andrea Milford, my best friend. ♥♥♥♥
   We've had our ups and downs as friends, but I hope we'll be friends forever.

6. Chip McKinnon, the guy I like. ♥♥♥♥
   Chip's cute, funny, and best of all, dependable.

7. Tom Harris, my new stepfather. I hated him at first, but since he went out and got Dribbles for me, I guess he's not too bad. Time will tell.

8. Nick Harris, my new stepbrother. Nick's in tenth grade at a fancy prep school. I think he's spoiled—a lot! But so far, he's been OK.

9. Jacob Benton, or Uncle Jacob. ♥♥♥
   I don't know how we're related, but we are. Maybe he's my stepuncle or something. He's gruff and tough and runs the big Harris house. I really like him.

1

"So how was your mom's honeymoon?"

"Huh?" I forgot for a moment that I was talking to my best friend. My puppy, Dribbles, was chewing the tassels on my new leather shoes, a Christmas present from my new stepfather.

Andrea gave an exasperated sigh. "Honestly, Cassie, are you off in space or something? I asked about your mom's honeymoon."

"It was OK, I guess," I said, falling back on my bed and lifting my feet away from Dribs. I propped the telephone against my pillow so I could examine my nails. "Mom came home in a good mood."

"I'd be in a good mood, too, if I'd spent my honeymoon in Hawaii." Andrea sighed. "Cassie Perkins, you don't know how lucky you are. Now you've got a gorgeous big brother—"

"*Step*brother."

"OK, a gorgeous stepbrother, a genius little brother, a cute boyfriend, and Mr. Moneybags for a stepfather. And the old guy—what's his name?"

"Uncle Jacob."

"Uncle Jacob does all the work around the house so you don't have to. All the men in your life are great. What else could you want?"

I sighed. Andrea would never understand. The past year of my life had been terrible. My parents had split up, Max and I had been separated, I had gone to a new school and hated it. Then we had to move out of our house, Mom got married again, and Suki, my wonderful, favorite dog, had been killed. And Andrea thought I was lucky?

"I want just one thing," I told her. "All I want is to start the new year fresh and try to be normal for a change."

"If you're really coming back to the old gang at Astronaut High, you'll be getting normal, all right. It's so normal, it's boring."

I couldn't help smiling. "Sounds great to me."

I was more nervous on the first day of second semester at Astronaut High than I had ever been. I was tempted to tell Mom I was sick, but I didn't think she'd buy it. I smoothed the fabric of my new skirt (a Christmas present supposedly from Nick, but I knew better) and picked at my bangs so they wouldn't clump together.

I stepped back, looked in my mirror, and groaned.

I'd been away from the kids at Astronaut for seven months, and there had been a lot of changes in my life. Plus, I'd never been to high school. Astronaut Junior High had been small and friendly. The School for the Performing Arts had been small, too. But more than two thousand kids went to Astronaut High, and I didn't even know how to find my locker. If it weren't for Andrea and Chip, I would never have found the nerve to go back.

A horn tooted from the driveway. "Hurry up, Cass," Mom called from downstairs. "Tom's ready to go."

"Coming!" I yelled over the banister. Dribs was sleeping in his little doggie bed, so I gave him a final good-bye scratch on his belly and gathered my notebook and purse. At the door, I closed my eyes and whispered a quick prayer: *"Help!"*

Astronaut High was a sprawling campus of concrete-block buildings and what seemed like miles of sidewalks. "We only have six minutes between classes?" I whispered to Andrea as Tom drove us around the school property. "How do you ever get anywhere on time?"

Andrea rolled her eyes. "Honestly, Cassie, it's just school. You'll get used to it."

Tom stopped the Mercedes in front of the office.

"If they have any questions, have them call me at work," he told me as we got out. "And have a good day, Cassie."

I mumbled something that sounded pleasant and got out of the car. As he pulled away, Andrea looked at me. "Do you like him better now?" she asked.

I watched the car until it disappeared. Tom Harris was trying his best to be nice to me because he really loved my mom. He had agreed to let me go back to Astronaut and had even promised to pay for my private voice lessons since I wouldn't be getting them at school anymore. I knew all that. But he would never be my father, no matter how hard he tried.

"I don't hate him anymore," I said finally, pulling at a stubborn strand of hair that kept falling into my eyes. I turned toward the office. "Come on, let's get on with this."

Miss Clarence, the guidance counselor, filled out a schedule form and gave it to me. "Now for your locker." She looked through several desk drawers and finally stood up. "It's been so long since we had a new student I nearly forgot where I keep these things," she joked as she searched through her filing cabinet. "Here we are. There's an empty locker in the new section in the east wing. Be sure to memorize the combination."

I took the paper and heard a bell ring. "That's the

warning bell," Miss Clarence said, smiling. "If you girls hurry along, I won't need to write you a pass to class."

We left her office and headed out into the hall. Andrea rolled her eyes. "Rats. I was hoping we would be late."

"Not me." I was so nervous I was out of breath. "If we're late, everyone will stare at us. Let's hurry."

I clutched my notebook, lowered my head, and pushed through the crowd with Andrea trailing behind me. I saw a few familiar faces and heard a few greetings:

"Hey, Cassie, where you been?"

"Cassie Perkins! What happened to you?"

I waved to a few kids I knew. I noticed other kids simply nodding toward me and then whispering to their friends. Some people probably didn't even know I had been gone.

"Slow down," Andrea complained, trying to keep up. "You're not going to have any social life if you don't stop and talk to some of these people."

A tall, red-haired boy I recognized stared at me as I passed, probably trying to remember where I'd been or who I was. "My social life can wait," I mumbled. "Right now, I just want to find room 112."

"You're with me," Andrea sighed. "Freshman

English. Miss Chamberlain. It's boring. All she does is read poetry."

"I like poetry," I said, walking faster.

Andrea crinkled her nose. "You're weird, Cass. Anyway, remember Tommy McLaughlin?"

"Wasn't he the red-haired guy we just passed?"

"It's orange, Cassie. The dweeb has orange hair. Anyway, he puts his head down and sleeps through class every morning. Last week Eric Brandt tore a piece of paper into a little circle and put it on top of Tommy's head while he was sleeping. Then Eric passed a note around that said, 'Tommy and Bozo are identical twins.' It was hilarious!"

"Didn't the teacher see him?" I said, thinking of the strict teachers at my old school.

"Are you kidding?" Andrea laughed. "Once Miss Chamberlain starts to read a poem, she never takes her eyes out of the book. Eric and his friends can get away with anything!"

I rushed into room 112 with Andrea behind me. She pointed to an empty desk across from hers, and I slipped into it with relief.

"You see?" Andrea complained as I tried to catch my breath. "We've got three whole minutes to spare. There's not even anyone here yet. Besides," she said, winking at me. "You could have spent that time talking to Chip."

"I haven't even seen Chip yet."

"You will. He's in this class, too."

Chip is my boyfriend, I guess. I like him better than any other guy I've known, and Andrea's always telling me how lucky I am that he likes me, too. But we're really more like best friends than a mushy couple. He's always been there when I've needed him, and I really do love him. But I'm not exactly sure that I want to marry him or anything.

Kids began to straggle in, and just as the tardy bell sounded, Chip burst through the door. He smiled at Miss Chamberlain, then took a quick glance around the room. He saw me, smiled, and came my way. I could feel my cheeks turning red.

"I'm sorry I'm late," he whispered, sliding into the desk behind me. "I wanted to meet you at the office, but I overslept. My uncle and I were up most of the night with a sick basset hound."

Chip loves animals, especially dogs, and since last summer he's been helping out at his uncle's veterinarian's office. "It's OK," I whispered, smiling over my shoulder and thinking how great it was going to be to have my two best friends in my first period class. I held up my schedule card. "Everything's all arranged."

Chip took my schedule and looked it over. "Sorry, Cassie," he whispered. "Looks like this is the only class we have together. But we eat lunch at the same time, so I'll meet you in the cafeteria."

"OK," I whispered back. Then Miss Chamberlain cleared her throat loudly and began checking attendance. A couple of kids twittered in the back of the room as a spitball went sailing past Tommy McLaughlin's head. Miss Chamberlain looked up, frowned, and looked around for guilty faces.

I loved it. It was good to be back where I belonged.

2

I couldn't help but notice that Andrea spent most of her time with her head turned toward Eric Brandt. She must have tossed her blonde hair in his direction a hundred times, and whenever he said something under his breath or made fun of Miss Chamberlain or Tommy McLaughlin, Andrea OD'd on giggles.

Eric seemed to be putting on a show, and I knew it had to be for Andrea. No one else paid him any attention, except for his two best friends, who nodded and muttered, "All right!" whenever he said something they thought was particularly witty.

Miss Chamberlain was oblivious to it all. She opened her book and announced that she would read a line from Robert Herrick: "What is a kiss?" she read.

Eric made a loud, smacking sound. Andrea covered her mouth and giggled. Tommy McLaughlin snored.

"What is a kiss?" Miss Chamberlain repeated, apparently not seeing or hearing anything in the classroom. "Why this, as some approve: The sure, sweet cement, glue, and lime of love."

Miss Chamberlain lowered her book. "The poet is using a metaphor," she said. "He is comparing a kiss to what?" She looked around the room. "Anyone?"

No one raised a hand. Andrea looked demurely down at her desk. Eric turned sideways in his desk and gazed at Andrea. Chip was jiggling his legs behind me, trying to stay awake. I raised my hand.

"Yes?" Miss Chamberlain said, nodding at me. "What is your name again?"

"Cassie Perkins," I said. "And he's comparing a kiss to cement or glue. It's what sticks people together."

Eric threw back his head and whooped, and Andrea giggled. I felt my cheeks burning. What was so funny? It was the right answer, and why should I sit there and pretend to be a dummy? And why was my best friend laughing at me, too? I looked over at Andrea and glared. She looked away and smiled at Eric Brandt.

"That's very good, Cassie." Miss Chamberlain nodded. "And Mr. Brandt, since you find this so funny, perhaps you can explain the humor in the situation?"

Eric didn't answer, he just turned slightly toward Miss Chamberlain and cocked his head. "Nothing," he said, smiling at her. He raised his chin and nodded like some kind of a king granting favors. "Go on with what you were doing."

The class got quiet—Andrea stopped twirling her hair in midair, Chip's legs stopped swinging, and Tommy McLaughlin even stopped snoring. Miss Chamberlain's eyes narrowed, and her knuckles whitened around the spine of the book she held in her hand. I figured she was struggling with the urge either to scream or to bash Eric Brandt with her poetry book. Finally, though, she opened the book again and kept reading. Everyone went back to normal, and Eric tossed Andrea a triumphant glance.

Andrea giggled and turned in her chair so that she faced him. I was feeling a little sick. What did Andrea Milford see in Eric Brandt? He was tall, dark-haired, and handsome in a reckless sort of way, but he was such a jerk! He had just treated Miss Chamberlain with a complete lack of respect. I couldn't believe he'd gotten away with it.

Miss Chamberlain closed her book at the end of class, and we gathered our books together to wait for the bell. I turned around to whisper to Chip. "When did Eric Brandt become such a brat?"

Chip shrugged. "He's always been that way, Cassie. You just didn't know him before."

Andrea was leaning in my direction now. "What

do you have next period, Cass?" she asked. "Need help finding the room?"

I turned toward her. "No thanks," I said coolly. "I'm a big girl. I think I can find my way around."

Andrea raised an eyebrow in surprise, then she jerked her head away. "Suit yourself." She turned to talk to Eric but not before casting a triumphant smile in my direction.

Great. I'd changed schools to be with my friends, and I'd lost my best friend after exactly one hour. What was wrong with me?

The science lab was locked up, so I stood outside on the sidewalk to wait for Mr. McClain, the teacher for freshman biology. The other girls were talking in small, confidential groups, and a few of the boys were running around on the grassy lawn. The freshmen boys' immaturity really showed, especially when I compared them to the seniors.

A group of seniors came through the hall, walking slowly and regally. We freshmen cleared a path for them, but we watched everything they did. A couple came by, holding hands and walking slowly, then came a group of football players, their shoulders as broad as billboards. I leaned back against the building, a little self-conscious.

I could see a teacher coming, a short, absent-minded-professor type with a stack of books and a circle of about fifty keys in his free hand. He was so intent on his key search that he bumped into a group of senior girls who were waiting outside the classroom next door.

He was embarrassed. They were all taller than he was, and a very pretty dark-haired girl nodded toward him as he walked away. "Clumsy McClain," she said, loud enough for everyone to hear. "Remember how boring he was in biology?"

The other girls giggled and the teacher walked more quickly toward our door, still fumbling with his keys. So, he was my biology teacher. I stepped away from the door and looked down at the ground, pretending I hadn't heard anything.

Holly Musgrave, a quiet, serious girl I'd known in seventh grade, was waiting against the wall, too. "Who was that girl?" I asked, nodding my head toward the dark-haired girl who had embarrassed Mr. McClain.

"That's Melanie Sergeant," Holly whispered. "She's been really nasty to everyone this year. Last semester she was suspended for ten days because she threw a book at a teacher."

"Wow." I looked over at the older girls again, as they slowly moved into their classroom.

"Yeah," Holly whispered. "My sister says Melanie used to be the queen bee around here. She was the most popular, captain of the cheerleading squad, the works. She wanted to be homecoming queen with a passion."

"What happened?"

Holly raised an eyebrow. "Arien Belle happened. Arien's a new girl from California, and she's beautiful, nice, and really cool. Everyone likes her. She won homecoming queen, she's dating Payton—"

"Who's Payton?"

"Just the best-looking, most wonderful guy in school, that's all," Holly said, shaking her head as if she couldn't believe how ignorant I was. "Boy, you really have been out of it, haven't you, Cassie?"

"In a different world," I said, crinkling my nose. "But I'm back now. So, what does this Arien look like? I don't think I've seen her."

"You'd know her if you saw her," Holly said. "She's really unusual looking. She looks like she's twenty. Blonde. Blue eyes. Gorgeous."

"Great." I shook my head and pretended to be discouraged. "Unfair competition for short, dark-haired people like me."

Holly snickered. "There is no competition, Cassie. No one, not even Melanie Sergeant, can come close to competing with Arien Belle."

We heard the click of the lab door—Mr. McClain had finally found the right key. I leaned closer to whisper to Holly. "So Melanie Sergeant must hate Arien Belle, right?"

"No," Holly whispered as we filed into the lab. "Everyone likes Arien. If Melanie didn't hang around Arien and her friends, Melanie wouldn't have anyone. Say . . ." Holly was about to climb onto the lab stool next to me, but she paused. "Where's Andrea? Didn't you get in all her classes?"

I shook my head. "No. Go on, sit there. She's not in this class. Besides," I whispered, "I think she's in love. She doesn't have time for her friends."

"I heard about her and Eric Brandt." Holly put her books on the table and hopped up on the stool. "My sister's in eleventh grade, and she's in love, too. With a senior." She opened her biology book, and I knew our conversation was over. Holly was a serious student, not the type to fill me in on the latest gossip in class. But she did look over once more: "Welcome back," she said simply.

My last class was in the gym. I wasn't wild about it, but it was the only opening in physical education, and Miss Clarence had insisted I take it. "Figure improvement is a fun, easy class," she had said, writing it on my schedule card. "You'll enjoy it."

Sure. Figure improvement—I didn't really have much of a figure to start with. I was short, which meant everything I ate usually went to my stomach.

"Honey, you're a carpenter's dream," my dad told me once. "Flat as a board." That hurt, and later I cried about it. I know Dad didn't mean to make me feel bad, but he did.

Now I was in high school, surrounded by senior girls who were built like Greek statues. Slim, but with curves in all the right places. I'd *never* look like them.

Since I didn't have gym clothes yet, I was relieved to see that we weren't dressing today. All the girls in my class came into the gym and sat on the bleachers, mostly in small groups, but I sat by myself and looked around. There were several girls who were a little overweight, probably hoping to lose a few pounds. There were a couple of skinny girls that looked even more like plywood than I did. All in all, we were a pitiful-looking group of ninth graders.

Mrs. Simmons came out of the office when the bell rang, a typical gym teacher: tall, skinny, and with a clipboard permanently attached to her left hand. She blew on a whistle for quiet and yelled like a Marine sergeant: "Ladies, group together, please!"

We all groaned and moved to the center section of the bleachers. I saw Leah Stiles, a familiar face from junior high, and sat next to her. She looked at me curiously, probably wondering like everyone else why I wasn't with Andrea.

Miss Simmons called the roll, then put the clipboard down and nodded enthusiastically. "Figure improvement is a course designed to contour and strengthen the muscles," she recited loudly. "The exercises we do will encourage muscle strength and flexibility. Plus, it will keep you from being bent over when you're sixty."

Was that a joke? No one laughed.

She put a foot up on the first bleacher and leaned forward on her knee. "I could talk all day," she said, losing her drill sergeant voice and speaking more like an ordinary teacher. "But let me show you."

She blew her whistle and from somewhere in the gym we heard music, a lively, rhythmic song. Then, from out of Miss Simmon's office, a girl appeared and began moving across the gym floor.

She was probably about twenty-one, maybe a teacher's aide. She whirled through a routine on the gym floor that left all of us breathless and a little scared—were *we* supposed to do *that?* At first I thought she was dancing, but then I realized her routine was structured. It was ordinary exercises, but nothing about the way she did them was ordinary. She made it look like fun, though, and as she whirled, her blonde ponytail bouncing, I wanted to climb down there and do it, too.

With a flourish of her arms and a toss of her head,

the music ended. We all burst into spontaneous applause, and Miss Simmons smiled. "You see, girls," she said. "Figure improvement can be fun." Miss Simmons nodded to the blonde girl, who was wiping her face with a towel. "Can you say something to inspire them for me?"

"Sure," the girl said, and she walked over to us. "If you want to be your absolute best, you've got to work at it." Her eyes sparkled with energy. "Everyone has a dream, and everyone has a gift. It's your job to find your gift and your dream, and do everything you can to make those dreams come true. You can't do it by sitting home and watching TV and eating Ding Dongs. You've got to get out and do something with yourself!"

I bit my lip as she talked. I knew *exactly* what she was talking about. It was my dream of becoming a singer that had led me to audition for the starring role in *Oklahoma!* in eighth grade. It was that same dream that led me to the School for the Performing Arts. I still wanted to be a singer—that's why I was taking private voice lessons. Not many people understood how my dream had driven me—but this girl obviously did.

"Well, this class can help you get off to a good start," the girl said. "I'm a senior, and I don't need any more physical education classes, but I'm taking this one because you can't get lazy if you want to be in the best possible physical shape."

"Thank you," Miss Simmons told the girl, then she looked at us. "Tomorrow bring your gym clothes and running shoes and be prepared to work!"

She walked away, leaving us to talk until the bell rang, and I turned to Leah. "That girl is a student?" I asked.

She looked at me as if I'd come from Mars. "You don't know Arien?" she asked, raising an eyebrow. "Good grief, Cassie. Where have you been?"

I ignored Leah and looked around to see where Arien had gone. It wasn't hard to spot her. A guys' class had come into the gym, and their faces were like searchlights, all shining toward Arien. She wasn't hanging around the guys, though. She was on the far side of the gym, her back toward me, talking to someone on the bleachers. Who? I was dying of curiosity.

I couldn't see at first, but then she reached out, patted the someone on the knee, and turned to go into the girls' locker room. Good grief! I couldn't believe it. She had been talking to Tommy Mc-Laughlin, the resident geek of our freshman class. What could they possibly have in common?

3

My mom had the usual twenty questions when I got home. She is always redecorating something, and she must have had a new project in mind because she was in the library, looking at fabric swatches. But she put everything down to ask if I liked my classes.

"They were OK."

Was I with Andrea much?

"Enough." (I didn't tell her Andrea would rather impress a stupid guy than be loyal to her best friend.)

Did I see Max? "No, not once. He's in all the genius classes, Mom. I'm with the regular kids."

Did I have any classes—she winked at me—with Chip? "Just one, Mom. But we ate lunch together."

"That's good, honey."

I walked to the kitchen to get a Coke, and when the refrigerator door creaked, I heard Uncle Jacob bellow from the dining room: "Who's in the fridge? No snacking! You'll spoil your appetite!"

"It's just me, Uncle Jake," I called, popping the top

of my Coke can. "And I have to have a Coke after school. It's a requirement."

He came into the kitchen then, his usual unlit cigar stub clenched between his teeth. "Whose requirement?" he muttered. "That stuff will stunt your growth, Missy." His dark eyes scanned my face, and I knew that underneath all his gruffness he was really concerned. "Nice day?" he growled.

I shrugged. "I guess so. The kids are just like they were in junior high, only—"

"What happened?" Uncle Jacob snapped.

I sat on the barstool at the counter. "Andrea's my best friend, remember? But she likes this guy named Eric, and she laughed at me just to impress him."

Uncle Jacob wrinkled his forehead. "Isn't she the boy-crazy one I met at the wedding? Seems she was flirting with Nick all night."

"She'll flirt with anyone. But she's liked Eric all year, I guess, and now he's beginning to notice." I took a swig of my Coke. "I mean, I have a boyfriend, but I don't ignore her."

Uncle Jacob leaned on the kitchen counter and growled. "And how is the wonderful Chip Mc-Kinnon these days? As wonderful as ever?"

"He's fine." I looked up and smiled. "But I only see him in one class and at lunch."

"I see." Uncle Jacob took the cigar stub out of his

mouth and held it between his fingers. He stopped smoking years ago, but sometimes he absently flicks his cigar stub as if it were really lit. "Sounds like school can be pretty lonely on the first day. Isn't there anyone you can pal around with?"

I laughed. "Really, Uncle Jake, a *pal?* There are a few girls in my classes that I knew in junior high, but they all expect me to hang around with Andrea."

"Give it some time, Missy." Uncle Jacob straightened up and moved toward the stove. Something that smelled delicious was simmering in a big pot, and he walked over to stir it. "You'll find a friend, or Andrea will come back to her senses. You've got my word on it."

By Friday morning, I still hadn't found any new friends. Acquaintances, sure. But friends? That's one problem with going to school with people you've known since kindergarten. They're all stuck in their friendship ruts, and no one's about to break out of them. If I had known in kindergarten that I was going to be assigned to Andrea for life, well—I don't know what I'd have done.

Eric met Andrea before school, ate with her at lunch, and walked her home after school. She's liked guys before, but this was the first time she's ever really gone with anybody. It was like she expected the world to stand still and notice that "Eric likes

Andrea." I even got over being mad at her and tried to be friendly, but she just didn't have time for me anymore.

"Ignore her," Chip told me at lunch on Friday. "She'll see someone new, break up with Eric, and it'll all be over. You know Andrea, Cassie. This won't last long."

Maybe Chip was right, but it didn't make me feel any better. If Chip had been around more, maybe I wouldn't have been alone so much, but he went straight to his uncle's animal hospital after school, and so there wasn't any time besides lunch and before school for me to see him. At night, he had too much homework to talk very long on the telephone, and Andrea never called me anymore.

I couldn't even hang around my own brother. Marvelous Max, as the teachers called him, kept his ten-year-old genius self either in the biology lab or the computer lab, where he entertained his teachers. I did see him in the halls once or twice, but he was usually being hounded by some football player for tutoring. Max was very popular with the kids on the athletic teams. When their grades went down, Max was the first person they called. He had turned into some kind of unofficial team mascot, Astronaut High's littlest astronaut.

On Friday afternoon, after a disastrous week at

school, I hung around the gym until the after-school rush had left. It was just too depressing to walk through the halls when everyone was laughing with, yelling at, or whispering secrets to someone else. I went to my locker, one of the new ones down a forgotten hall far away from people who had friends. "The outcast lockers," I muttered, walking to mine.

My locker was on the bottom row, and I knelt on the hard floor, trying to remember which teachers had been cruel enough to give us homework over the weekend. The rattle of another locker startled me, and I looked up to see Arien Belle opening the locker above mine. "Sorry," she said, opening the door carefully so she wouldn't hit my head. "I'll just be a minute."

How did a senior get a locker out here in the forgotten-freshman zone? Then I remembered—Arien was a new student too. Wow. I suddenly realized my mouth was open in amazement, so I looked down and snapped it shut. What could I say to her? I couldn't just sit here like a dummy.

"Sorry," I echoed her words. "I'm sorry I'm in the way."

"You're not," she said, and she looked down at me and smiled. She was so pretty, and not just cover-girl pretty, either. There was something unusual in her eyes; she actually looked *interested,* and she seemed to study me for a minute. "You're in my gym class, aren't you?"

"Huh?" I hadn't been listening. I'd been wondering if she wore contacts or if her eyes really were aqua.

She laughed. "My gym class. Figure improvement? You're in there, right?"

I nodded. "Yeah. I'm Cassie Perkins."

I'm sure she knew she didn't need to tell me *her* name, but she did, anyway. "I'm Arien Belle. If I can just grab my English book, I'll be out of your way."

"Sorry." I ducked my head and she lifted a heavy book out of her locker, then gave the door a definite slam.

"See you, Cassie."

"'Bye."

I was watching my usual Saturday afternoon creature feature on TV when Nick came into the den, picked up the remote, and—without asking—changed the channel to ESPN. I couldn't believe it.

"What do you think you're doing?" I asked him. "I was watching something."

Nick glared at me. "That was just a stupid movie," he said. "I've seen it twenty times. We *always* watch sports here on the weekends."

"That's not fair." I sat up, ready to defend my rights. "I'll call my mother!"

"I'll call my father," Nick replied, settling back in the easy chair. "We'll see who wins then."

"I had the TV first!"

"So?"

"Mom!" I felt kind of stupid, yelling for my mother like a little kid, but I didn't know what else to do. Max heard me yell and stuck his head into the room.

"What's wrong, Cassie?"

I glared at Nick. "This guy is *impossible* to live with! But I wouldn't expect you to understand because you're the lucky one! You only have to come over here every other weekend."

Max looked at Nick. "I like Nick," he said simply. "I wouldn't mind living with him all the time. And I'd like to watch ESPN, too."

Nick put his hand out and Max gave him a high five. That did it. Max's association with all those jocks had ruined his brain. I ran upstairs to my mother's room, yelling the entire way that life with brothers was unjust and certainly unfair.

Mom was trying to take a nap, so her quick and easy solution was to get me out of the house. Tom would give me fifty dollars, take me to the mall, and pick me up promptly at four o'clock. I was still mad at Nick and a little upset that Max had sided with the enemy, but having a rich stepfather had its good points. "Don't you have someone to go with you?" Mom called from her bedroom window as I got into the car. "Call Andrea and see if she wants to go, too."

"Don't worry, Mom, I'll be OK," I said, buckling my seat belt. "I'll meet Tom right on time, and no one's going to kidnap me."

Mom waved as we pulled out of the driveway, but her parting words echoed in my head: "Just don't waste that money, OK?" Until she married Mr. Moneybags, there hadn't been any money to waste.

4

No one had ever given me money before without strict instructions about how to spend it. Usually if I got money for my birthday or Christmas, Mom and Dad made me use it for something I needed like clothes, underwear, or movie money. I wasn't used to being allowed to buy whatever I wanted.

I stopped for a minute by the fountain in the mall and tried to think. What should I get? A record? A book? A hat? Clothes? I remembered an aqua sweater Arien Belle had worn to school a couple of days ago. It was soft, like cashmere, and came off the shoulder. On her, it was gorgeous, highlighting her delicate skin and her eyes. On me, it would probably look stupid, but maybe I could find something like it.

I stepped into The Gap and found a table loaded with sweaters similar to Arien's. I had two in my hand, one red and one black, when I heard a faintly familiar voice: "You know, the red one would look great on you."

I looked up, and there in front of me were Arien

Belle and Melanie Sergeant. Arien was smiling, but Melanie had her arms folded and was looking off into space, obviously bored.

"The red one?" I put the black one down.

Arien took the red one, shook it out, and held it up in front of me. "What do you think, Mel?" she asked. "Doesn't it look great with her dark eyes?"

Melanie rolled her eyes. "Sure, Arien. Can we hurry up here? We'll be late, you know."

"The black one would be nice, too, but I vote for the red one," Arien smiled again. "You're Cassie, right?"

I nodded stupidly.

"Shopping?"

I nodded again.

"Alone?"

I finally found my voice, but it came out in a pitiful squeak. "Yes."

Arien jerked her head toward Melanie. "Why don't you get your sweater and come with us? We're meeting some other girls at the four o'clock movie. Want to come?"

Did I want to come? Of course! I'd cut off my right arm to go with them. Imagine me, Cassie Perkins, with a group of senior girls, hanging out in the mall. Andrea would die, and so would the rest of the freshman class!

But it was three-thirty, and Tom would be waiting for me in half an hour. If I was late, Mom would have the police out looking for me for sure.

"Um, I don't know," I said, embarrassed. Seniors were old enough to have cars and didn't have to check with their parents to do everything. But if I could meet Tom, and tell him to come back at six, I could go. "Can I meet you there? I, uh, still have some shopping to do."

"Sure. We'll look for you." Arien waved and walked out, but Melanie lingered. She closed her eyes and shook her head slowly. "I don't believe her," she muttered, then she turned in my direction and hissed, "Don't be late." Then she followed Arien out of the store, wondering loudly why Arien had to pick up "every stray in the mall."

I didn't care about Melanie. She was just jealous and sour. I picked up the red sweater and headed toward the cash register. If I hurried, this could be the most important day of my entire freshman year.

"Sorry," Tom said when I met him by the mall entrance. "Jacob said dinner was at five-thirty, and your mom and I have something special we want to do with you kids tonight. I can't leave you here until six."

I couldn't believe what I was hearing. He wouldn't

let me stay? Didn't he realize how important this was to me?

"Tom," I began slowly, "this is *really* important. These are really nice girls, and we're not doing anything wrong. We're just going to a movie, for heaven's sake."

"No, Cassie, I'm afraid not." Tom took my package and started for the door.

I took two steps and then stopped. "I'll bet they could give me a ride home," I offered hopefully. "Arien has her own car, and I just know she'd take me home so you wouldn't have to come back. Please, Tom? I promise it will all work out."

Tom looked at me. "No, Cassie, I'm afraid not. First of all, your mother would kill me if I left you here without making sure that you had a ride home. I don't even know these girls."

"Arien's the most popular girl in school!" I whispered intensely, offended that he thought I'd hang out with troublemakers or something. "Don't you trust me? My mother trusts me."

Tom closed his eyes and shook his head. "Cassie, this is my last word and it is final. No, you cannot stay. Your mother and I have plans for the family tonight, and we want you to be there. Now come on."

I didn't move, and Tom didn't either. For what

seemed like a long time we just stood there, glaring at each other. I was thinking about making a break for the movie theater, and wondering if I'd be grounded for life if I tried. Tom looked like he was seriously considering throwing me over his shoulder and carrying me out the door.

"Then can I at least go tell my friends I can't come? They were going to wait outside the movie for me, and I don't want them to miss the start of the movie."

"No," Tom said again. "You shouldn't have told them you could come without checking with me first. Now we've taken too long as it is. Let's go."

He'd probably said no because he thought I might take off and not come back—and who knows, maybe I would have. But I gritted my teeth and stomped out of the mall, taking the biggest steps my midget legs could manage. If I had to leave, it wouldn't be with Tom. I ran out to the car, leaving Tom to follow after me.

Uncle Jacob had prepared a really wonderful din- ner with everyone's favorite foods: Lasagna for Nick, Italian bread for me, shrimp salad for Mom and Tom, and the promise of Twinkies for Max. I noticed one other weird thing, too: Mom was drinking milk. She had always been really strict about making me and Max drink milk at dinner, but now she and Nick were drinking it, too. I shrugged. She probably couldn't think of any other way to get Nick to drink milk at dinner, so she was setting a good example.

Everyone was in a good mood except me, of course. While everyone else joked and laughed, I was trying to figure out how I was going to explain to Arien why I couldn't go to the movie with her. How could I explain that my stepfather wouldn't let me stay at the mall? That he didn't trust them to bring me home? That I still had to *ask* for permission to do anything? Arien probably wouldn't even speak to me after this. It had been a once-in-a-lifetime chance, and I'd missed it.

After our dessert (Twinkies in chocolate sauce), Tom stood up and rapped the side of his glass of iced tea with a spoon. "Attention, please, everyone," he said, smiling. "We have some important news for this family, and we wanted to give it while we are all together."

Family. I wanted to gag on the word. This man was not my family. What was he trying to do?

I looked across the table at Max. He shrugged and looked at Nick. Nick raised his eyebrows and looked at Uncle Jacob. Uncle Jacob just grinned.

I figured whatever he was planning to announce must be good news because Tom, Mom, and Uncle Jacob seemed happy. Then it hit me—maybe they had somehow worked it out so Max would live here, too! I couldn't imagine Dad giving up custody of Max, but maybe Dad had had second thoughts since Mom had remarried. I held my breath.

"There are going to be changes in the Harris household," Tom said in his lawyer voice. "We're all going to have to make a few sacrifices to make room for one more."

Of course! Nick was going to have to share his room with Max. I looked over at Max and tried to kick him under the table. I don't know how they arranged it, but I would love to have Max around.

"One more?" Nick said dully. The dummy! Didn't he get it?

"Yes," Tom said, nodding. "Claire is going to have a baby in September."

No. A baby? Not Max? It couldn't be. My mother was thirty-seven, and thirty-seven-year-old women with kids in high school don't have babies. Do they? In a daze, I looked at my mother, who sat in her chair, sipping her glass of milk. A baby? She and Tom were having a baby? It was crazy. Tom had gray hairs, for heaven's sake!

Nick whooped in delight. "That's great. I always wanted to be an uncle."

"You won't be an uncle, dunderhead," Uncle Jacob bellowed. "The baby will be your brother—"

"Or sister," Mom added.

Nick settled back in his chair, more than a little confused. Max spoke up next. In his calm and even voice, he said, "Mom, Tom, congratulations. I'm looking forward to this. Being the youngest child, I've never had the chance to experience a pregnancy on a personal level."

"Max," Mom said, shaking her head, "you're making me feel like a lab rat."

"Sorry," Max said. "But I think this is tremendous. New life! Fetal development! I think I'll dump all my tutoring so I'll have a chance to research pregnancy during the next few months."

"That's OK, Max," Mom said. "Keep tutoring."

Mom and Tom looked at me next. What did they want me to say? I knew they wouldn't want to hear what I was thinking. "Is this over?" I said, as politely as I could. "I missed something very important for this, so I'd like to be excused now."

Mom looked down at her plate and I could tell she was disappointed. Tom nodded to me, his expression serious. "You're excused," he said, but with that tone of voice he could have well said, "You're a total jerk."

I pushed back my chair and left the room. A baby! How gross! Everything I had ever heard about sex and pregnancy came flooding back to me, and I felt nauseated. Didn't Mom know anything about birth control? Surely they couldn't have planned to have a baby!

Running up the stairs, I went into my room, slammed the door, and slid into a heap on the floor. A baby! If it was a boy, it would end up in Nick's room. If it was a girl—I'd have to share my room. In either case, I'd probably become a permanent baby-sitter. My personal life would cease to exist for the next ten years.

I closed my eyes and tried to imagine a crib over in the corner. There was no way a baby was going to fit into my life.

What would my friends think? What would my teachers say when Mom showed up for meetings at school with her belly two feet out in front?

I put my hands over my flaming cheeks as the worst thought of all hit me: what would my father think?

5

Back at school on Monday, I was almost afraid to go to my locker. What if I bumped into Arien? How would I explain why I had just disappeared at the mall? The truth would sound just too ridiculous: my stepfather made me go home so we could hear the announcement that he and my mother were going to have a baby. Who'd believe that?

I had to tell somebody, though. I walked through the halls in a daze and finally spotted Chip at his locker. "Guess what?" I said, leaning my head against his shoulder.

"What?" I had startled him, and he took a step away from me.

"My mother's having a baby."

"*Your* mother's having a baby?"

"Yes. My mother's having a *baby*. Can you believe that?"

Chip's eyes were open wide, and I could tell he didn't really know how to react. "So? What does that mean?"

"Ugh, don't you realize? My mother, who's too old in the first place, will be walking around fat— something she's never been—and goo-gooing over baby clothes for the next eight months! And Tom will be the father!" I shuddered. "I can't handle this."

Chip laughed at me. "Cassie, you're crazy." He pulled his English book out of his locker. "It'll be fun. You'll probably have a ball with the kid."

He slammed the locker door and was about to take my hand and walk me to English. "No, you go ahead," I said, pulling back. "I haven't been to my locker yet."

"I'll go with you."

"No, you go ahead." I didn't want him to know I was hiding from Arien. "It's almost time for the bell, and there's no reason why both of us should be late." I took off toward my locker before he could argue.

I peeked around the corner to make sure Arien and her friends weren't around. They weren't, so I knelt, opened my locker, grabbed my English book, and was nearly done when in the corner of my eye I saw someone kneel next to me.

It wasn't Arien. It was Melanie Sergeant. "Where'd you run off to the other day?" she asked, smiling. "We waited for you, you know. We nearly missed the beginning of the movie."

"Sorry," I said, closing my locker and standing up. "But something came up, and I had to go."

"Oh." Melanie stood up too, smoothing her skirt. "Well, since you and Arien are so tight, I thought I'd let you in on a surprise. But you have to promise not to tell a soul."

I couldn't believe it. Melanie Sergeant was standing here, in public, about to tell me a secret. If only Andrea or one of those other girls could see this!

"We're giving Arien a surprise birthday party at the Southland Roller Rink," Melanie said, her dark eyes dancing. "It's Wednesday afternoon, after school, at four o'clock. Can you make it?"

I pretended to think carefully, as if I had a million things to do after school. "Yes, I can," I finally said. "Sure."

"If you get there and it looks deserted, don't worry," Melanie said, gently fingering her long hair. "We're all parking down the block and walking over to the rink. Arien's coming at four, so be a little early if you can, OK?"

"OK," I said with a nod.

"It'll be a great party," Melanie said. The bell rang and she walked away quickly. "Don't forget, and don't breathe a word to *anyone*, OK?"

"Sure." I waved and turned to run to class. I'd probably be late and have to go to the office for a tardy slip, but it would be worth it. I had another once-in-a-lifetime chance, and I wouldn't miss this one for anything!

On Tuesday afternoon, Mom took me to the mall so I could shop for a present for Arien. I went straight to The Gap because I knew Arien shopped there. Surely I could find something she'd like.

"You haven't told me just who this girl is," Mom said, glancing through a rack of dresses. "What is she like?"

"She's from California," I said, as if that explained it all. "She's really pretty, and sweet. Everyone loves her."

"Is she in ninth grade, too?"

I hadn't told Mom that Arien was a senior because I didn't know if she'd want me to hang out with older kids. "No, she's not," I said. "She looks really mature, though. If you saw her, you'd think she was at least twenty."

Mom raised an eyebrow. I picked up a sweater similar to the one I had bought, but this one was green with tiny golden sparkles throughout the weave. "What do you think, Mom? She's blonde, and her eyes are kind of blue-green."

"That would be nice. I'll take care of that for you." She smiled. "Tom gave me some money this afternoon, so we're all set." I ducked behind a rack of jeans and pretended to look through them, but I was really watching Mom as she paid for the sweater. She didn't look pregnant, at least, not yet. She was still slender and athletic looking, although today she was wearing jeans and a loose top instead of the classy jumpsuits she usually wore shopping. With her casual haircut and springy step, she could pass for thirty. Maybe being in public with her when she was pregnant wouldn't be too bad. People might think she was just a friend.

I had been dying to tell someone about the surprise party, but I knew I'd be forever blacklisted if I leaked the surprise. So I didn't tell Chip, who wouldn't really have cared, and I didn't even tell Andrea, who would have shriveled up and died in a jealous fit. I'd tell her *after* the party and watch her turn green with envy. Then she'd see what she had missed by spending all her time with Eric Brandt.

On Wednesday, all I could think about was the party. I was a pretty fair skater, so I knew I could at least skate around without falling and embarrassing myself to death. I pictured myself talking to Arien and Payton: "Oh, it's a lovely party, Arien. Maybe you and Payton can double sometime with me and Chip. We could get something to eat and see a movie."

She'd laugh and Payton would smile, and Chip would be so pleased that I'd set everything up. Everyone in the freshman class would be amazed that Cassie Perkins had become Arien Belle's best friend.

But I was nervous that afternoon when Tom dropped me off at the roller rink. "Are you sure there's a party here?" he asked, looking around at the parking lot. "There are only two cars here."

"Everyone parked down the block," I said, opening the car door. "And it's early yet, too. Arien won't be here for another fifteen minutes."

"OK," he said. I got out and Tom handed me the present, wrapped in the prettiest paper I could find. Arien would look gorgeous in the sweater, absolutely gorgeous. And every time she wore it, she'd tell people that Cassie Perkins gave it to her.

"I'll pick you up here at six o'clock," Tom said.

"Can you make it six-thirty?" I asked, leaning inside. "I can get something to eat at the snack bar, so it's not like I have to hurry home for dinner."

Tom nodded. Lately both he and Mom had gone out of their way to be nice to me. I knew they were just trying to help me accept Mom's pregnancy. "OK," Tom called, revving the engine. "See you then."

I waited until he pulled out of the parking lot,

then I walked to the double glass doors and tugged. Nothing. They were locked. I was probably *too* early.

There was a bench near a pay phone, so I walked over and sat down, feeling a little silly holding the big box wrapped in the spangly wrapping paper. I hoped no one drove by and recognized me.

For ten minutes I sat, growing more and more worried. Today was Wednesday, wasn't it? Melanie had said Wednesday, hadn't she? What if it was *next* Wednesday? No, surely she had meant this Wednesday.

She said four o'clock, after school. Well, it was four o'clock, it was after school, and I was at the roller rink. Wait a minute—had she said *which* roller rink? Canova Cove only had one rink, Southland, but what if she meant a rink in Cocoa Beach or even Melbourne?

No, no one would drive all the way to Cocoa Beach when there was a perfectly good rink right here in Canova Cove. Besides, she said the Southland Roller Rink, and here I was, at the Southland Roller Rink.

At two minutes till four, a car pulled in and Tommy McLaughlin got out. His hair was windblown from riding in the car and stood out on the sides. I had to bite my lip to keep from giggling. He really did look a little like Bozo, tall and leggy.

But what was he doing here? He wasn't carrying a present, either, just a pair of battered roller skates tied together by the laces. Tommy didn't even glance over at me but went to the double doors of the rink and pounded.

A man appeared and unlocked the door. Tommy said something to him, and the man propped the door open with a piece of cement block. Then the two of them disappeared behind the partition that separated the foyer from the rink.

The truth suddenly dawned on me. It was four o'clock and today was the right day. This was the right place, too, but there was no surprise party here. I remembered Melanie inviting me—her eyes had been dancing and her smile was bright, but not from excitement. She had been playing a trick on me. A low-down, rotten, dirty trick.

I stood up, my eyes filling with tears of frustration. How horrible! How mean could she be? Was it all to get back at me for not showing up at the movie on Saturday?

I walked to the pay phone, stuck in a quarter, and called home. The phone rang and rang. "Come on, Mom, Uncle Jacob, Nick, someone—answer!" There was no answer. I heard the answering machine click on and Tom's voice saying, "Hello, you've reached the Harris house. We're sorry no one is available to take your call now, but if you'll leave your name and number . . ." I hung up. They were all probably out somewhere doing something for the baby. And I would be stuck here until six-thirty.

I walked back to the bench and put my head down. When would I ever learn?

Another car pulled in, and this one actually stopped. I heard the door slam, then footsteps. The steps stopped, though, and someone said, "Cassie? Is that you? What are you doing here?" I looked up in surprise.

It was Arien! She was here, but she wasn't dressed for a birthday party. She was wearing a sweatsuit and, like Tommy, she was carrying a pair of roller skates.

"I, uh . . ." I tried to think of some way to explain without making myself sound stupid but couldn't think of anything. "I was told there was a surprise birthday party here today, but I must have confused the dates," I mumbled. "Pretty dumb, huh?"

Arien laughed. "There are never parties here in the afternoon. Afternoon hours are reserved for artistic skaters. Maybe the party you're invited to is tonight."

"Maybe." I looked away. "Thanks for stopping."

Arien didn't leave. "Are you stuck here?" she asked. "Do you need a ride home?

"No, my stepfather's coming at six-thirty," I said. "I can wait."

"Well, wait inside," Arien said, reaching for my arm and pulling me up. "The sun is too hot to sit out here. Besides, you can critique my performance."

"Your performance?"

Arien smiled as we walked in. "In figure skating. Everyone has a dream, you know, and this is mine."

6

The day was full of surprises. When we got inside, I
saw Tommy McLaughlin on skates in the rink. But
I'd never seen Tommy like this before. In school, he
was quiet, shy, and usually sleepy. But out on the
skating floor, he seemed tall, graceful, and powerful.
His glasses were off, and his red hair blew in the
breeze as he pumped with his skates, jumped,
twisted, and spun.

"Wow!" I watched with my mouth open. Arien
smiled as she shimmied out of her sweat pants and
top. Underneath she wore a short skating skirt and a
matching blouse. "He's good, isn't he?" she asked.
"He's my partner in the dance competition."

"You do this in competition?" I felt stupid. "Like
the ice skaters in the Olympics?"

Arien nodded. "Yes. Not many people know that
roller-skating has competition and levels just like ice
skating, but it does. And it requires just as much
work." She took off her shoes, slipped on her skates,
and began lacing them. "I practice every day for two

or three hours. You have to, if you want to be the best."

I was fascinated by the figure of Tommy McLaughlin on the rink. "I've known Tommy since kindergarten," I said quietly, "but I never knew he did *this*."

"Not many people do," Arien said, slipping a nylon cover over her skate. "Nobody really knows I skate, either. They don't understand. All my other friends would rather be cheerleaders or work or just hang out. Not me."

"I know how you feel," I said, looking at her. "I have an ambition, too." I could feel myself blushing. "Sort of."

"Really?" Arien stood up on her skates gracefully, but now she seemed at least five inches taller. "What is it?"

"Singing," I said, looking away. "I've been told I have some talent, and I want to be the best. But sometimes I get sidetracked."

"Take my word for it," Arien said, pushing off with one foot and gliding smoothly away. She yelled over to me: "It doesn't pay to get sidetracked. I'll tell you about it sometime."

Tommy and Arien skated and skated and skated. Mostly they stood on circles painted on the rink floor and skated figure eights over and over again. I couldn't believe how disciplined they were. Over and over again, without flinching, Arien stood on the tiny painted line, with its edges running squarely between the wheels of her skate. She'd bend her knees, push off, and on one foot glide effortlessly around the circle. Halfway through, she'd bring her free leg in front, and when she reached an adjoining circle, she'd push off and do the entire routine again, never once veering from off the painted circle.

After about half an hour of figure eights, the man who had unlocked the doors called them out of the rink. He was wearing skates now, too. He talked quietly to Tommy and Arien, often drawing figures in the air, then he skated over the carpeted floor to the sound booth and started the music as Tommy and Arien slid back onto the skating floor. It was basically unimaginative organ music, old tunes like "The Entertainer" and "The House of the Rising Sun," but Tommy and Arien didn't seem to care. They skated the same routine to whatever song came on.

The man, who they called Coach Davison, yelled at them from the sidelines: "Check the baseline! Pull those crosses in tighter, Tommy! Free leg straight and pointed, Arien!" None of it made any sense to me, but Tommy and Arien were obviously doing something right because they'd glide by, their heads up and smiling, and Coach Davison would clap in appreciation.

They were so graceful—Tommy stood behind Arien and to her left, holding her left hand in his, with his right hand on her right hip. They reminded me of those stiff little ceramic bride and groom figures on the tops of wedding cakes—always perfectly together, always perfectly straight.

They did four routines as Coach Davison called them out: the Harris Tango, the Rocker Foxtrot, the Carroll Tango, and the Silhouette Foxtrot. Finally the Coach yelled, "Take a break, kids," and Arien came skating my way. Tommy skated over to the snack bar.

"You are simply incredible," I said sincerely. "I've never seen anything like that on roller skates. I didn't know it was possible to do all that." I laughed. "Whenever I try anything fancy, my wheels get in the way."

Arien laughed too. "Want a Coke? Come on over to the snack bar and we'll get one. We can't have food over here in the spectators' section."

I followed her, feeling a little uncomfortable and shorter than ever because I was the only one in the building wearing shoes instead of skates. But Arien was babbling happily about competitions and spins and moves that Coach Davison had promised to teach her.

Coach Davison was behind the counter, and he winked at me and poured Cokes for us. "Glad to see these two have friends," he said, nodding toward Tommy and Arien. "I was beginning to wonder."

We slipped into a booth, and Arien stretched her long legs out on the seat and took a long sip through her straw. "Ah," she sighed. "I really get thirsty out there."

"You make it look so easy," I said. "I thought I was a decent skater until I saw you."

Arien smiled. "You probably make singing look easy, and I know it isn't," she said. "And since you've seen me skate, you've got to sing for me sometime."

I laughed and stirred my Coke with my straw. "Maybe."

"For sure," Arien said. "Fair is fair."

I tried to change the subject. "When did you get interested in skating, anyway?"

"In California," Arien said, looking out across the rink. "I was twelve years old and running with a really wild group. The kids were all a lot older than I was and into drugs and really heavy stuff."

She stopped to take a long drink, and I wondered if I was supposed to say something. But then she went on. "I nearly overdosed from heroin one time. I'd been shooting up with this guy who was a lot older, and I ended up in the hospital." She shook her head. "I can't really blame him, though. I told him I was seventeen, and he believed me. He didn't know I was just a kid."

"Wow."

"Yeah." She looked down at her skates, and her eyes were serious. "Anyway, my parents knew they had to do something or I'd end up killing myself. We couldn't move, so they put me in a detox center to clean out my system. After that, they signed me up with a skating coach."

She smiled again and the light came back to her eyes. "Well, skating did it for me. I finally found something that was fun, and that I was good at— and that was good for me. I won my first medal in the Junior Olympics level after my first year, and I was hooked."

She took another long sip of her drink then leaned her head on her hand, looking over at me. "Skating saved my life, Cassie. Really. Last year I won a silver medal in the California state competition, and my parents knew the best coach in the business was Terry Davison—he was a national champion in men's freestyle a few years ago. So Mom and I came out here to train this year with him. This year I want to win the national gold medal."

I was amazed. "Why doesn't anyone at school know all this?"

Arien shrugged. "No one wants to know. None of those girls at school know what it's like to work your tail off for something other than boyfriends or cheerleading. They're nice and all, but they have no idea what it means to have an ambition and really work hard at something. Tommy's the only kid I've ever met who even comes close, except, of course, for Payton." She dimpled. "He wants to go to med school and become a doctor, so I guess he counts."

I nodded toward Tommy, who had left the snack bar and was back practicing figure eights. "I never would have guessed that Tommy McLaughlin was an athlete," I said.

"He's shy," Arien said, standing up. "But he's really good. He won a gold medal at nationals last year in the Junior Olympics in figures."

"Those figure eights?" I pointed to him.

"Yes." Arien nodded. "I'm really lucky to have him for a dance partner."

Coach Davison called Arien over then, and she skated away. She worked on a different program with the coach while Tommy continued skating figure eights, over and over and over again.

When both Tommy and Arien looked as if they were about to drop, Coach Davison blew his whistle. "Do your victory laps and call it quits," he called. Arien skated over and stood near me for a minute, trying to catch her breath.

"I don't know why I'm so tired," she said, pausing between breaths. "Usually I can do twenty victory laps, but today I'll be lucky if I do ten."

"What are victory laps?"

She laughed. "Coach has this saying: 'On the day of victory, no one is tired.' You see, you can't get really strong unless you push yourself past the point where you're tired. So every day, before we go home, we skate fast laps just to build endurance. If we didn't call them victory laps," she said, taking a deep breath and pushing a few straggly hairs back up into her ponytail, "we'd probably call them suicide runs. Well, here goes."

She pushed off and skated away so fast I thought she'd crash into the walls as she rounded the corners. Tommy whizzed by, too, his skates whirring as he smoothly passed. I was startled when I felt a hand on my shoulder. "Cassie? Is the party over?" It was my mother.

"Oh." I looked away from the skaters and up at Mom. "There wasn't a party. Arien's here, but I must have confused the dates, so don't say anything, OK?"

She nodded. "Are you ready to go?"

"Yeah. But just a minute, Mom. Let me introduce you to Arien." As Arien skated by, I caught her eye by waving frantically. She skated over.

I introduced her to Mom, and Arien extended her hand. Mom shook it, smiled, and said it was nice to meet her.

"I've got to go now," I told Arien. "I've got a stack of homework to get through. But I really enjoyed watching you work."

"Come anytime." She smiled. "Sometimes it helps to have an audience. Seriously. I'm here every afternoon."

We left then, and I knew that I had made a new friend. Even my mother was impressed.

7

On Thursday morning I couldn't resist looking around for Melanie Sergeant. I couldn't let her think she'd tricked me.

I found her hanging around outside a classroom with two of her friends. Arien wasn't around, so I brazenly walked up to her side and edged my way into their circle.

"By the way, Melanie, I wanted to thank you for letting me know about yesterday at the roller rink," I said, smiling. "I had a wonderful time."

"Did you?" Melanie asked, bending her head down and smiling sweetly. "I missed the party myself. Was it a good crowd?"

I smiled back. "It was more like a gathering of close friends. But we had a great time."

Melanie cocked her head, a little confused, but just then Arien walked up. "Morning everybody," she said, then she saw me. "Cass! Did you get that stack of homework done?"

I laughed. "Yes, but I was up late doing it all. But

thanks again, Arien. I really enjoyed yesterday afternoon." I nodded at Melanie. "I've got to run now.
See you all later."

I laughed quietly as I walked away. Poor Melanie
would tear her hair out all morning, trying to figure
out what had happened yesterday.

Andrea actually took her eyes off Eric in English
long enough to talk to me. "Was that you I saw talking to Melanie Sergeant and Arien Belle this morning?" she asked, her eyes wide. "What was that
about?"

I shrugged. "Not much. Just the usual talk."

Andrea swung her legs around and leaned my
way. "When did you get to be friends with them?"

I rolled my eyes. "Honestly, Andrea, we all go to
the same school, you know."

"But they're *seniors*."

"So? Arien's in my gym class, and her locker's
above mine."

Andrea shook her head. "Honestly, Cassie. I never
thought you'd be so stuck up as to dump your best
friend for a bunch of seniors."

"What?" I couldn't believe what I was hearing. "I
didn't dump you—you dumped me! You haven't
had any time for me ever since you started going
with Eric. You don't even call me anymore."

Andrea flushed. "Why should I? You've been so grumpy lately no one wants to talk to you."

I turned away and folded my arms. Andrea was wrong, so why couldn't she see it? If I'd been grumpy at all, it was because my best friend didn't have time for me anymore.

Chip came in then, as usual beating the bell by five seconds. "Hi," he said, sliding into his seat behind me. "Sorry I didn't have time to call last night."

"It's OK," I whispered back over my shoulder. "I had homework, anyway." I looked over at Andrea, who was sulking. Carefully, so she could hear, I turned my head to the side. "Hey, Chip, how would you like to double-date sometime with Arien Belle and Payton Wardell?"

Andrea dropped her jaw and gaped at me, and even Chip was surprised. "Arien and Payton? Sure, maybe sometime." He leaned forward and whispered: "You're kidding, right?"

I turned back to the front of the room as Miss Chamberlain picked up her attendance notebook. When she looked down for a minute, I turned my head away from Andrea and whispered to Chip. "No, I'm not kidding," I said. "I can work it out."

That afternoon Uncle Jacob dropped me off at the skating rink. "Another party?" he asked.

"No," I said, gathering my books. "I just like being here. A couple of kids from school are in training, and I like to watch them. It's quiet here, too, and I can get my homework done."

"OK," Uncle Jacob answered. "One of us will swing by to get you at dinnertime, OK?"

"Thanks." He left, and I felt a sense of relief. The truth was, I just couldn't stand being around the house. Tom was always making baby jokes or tenderly putting his hand on Mom's belly, and I just couldn't stomach any more. They hadn't started buying baby clothes yet, but Mom tended to jabber on and on about her doctor, and how the baby was growing, and how different things were now compared to when she was pregnant with me and Max.

I was surprised when I walked into the rink, because today the place was humming with life. Tommy McLaughlin was still out on the rink skating his figure eights, but Arien was surrounded by five or six younger kids.

I went over to the snack bar, put my books down, and hopped up on the table to watch. Arien saw me and waved, but then she swooped her hands down quickly to catch a little girl who had just fallen on her rear. "Oops!" I heard Arien laugh. "Come on, Brittany, let's try that again!"

There was a pair of kids who looked like a miniature

68

version of Tommy and Arien. They skated as a pair, but they were probably only six or seven years old. I had to giggle when they went by—they were so young, but they looked so serious!

Little Brittany was apparently just learning to skate. She wore a tiny red skating skirt and white tights and had a gigantic red bow in her brown curls. She clip-clipped along, stepping instead of gliding, but she kept her arms out stiffly and her head up. There were a couple of younger boys, who were trying to get the hang of skating backward, and a red-haired girl, who looked about ten, was skating around and around the rink in some kind of routine.

Arien skated over and I heard the drag of her skate as she came to a stop. "Hey, Cassie. You came back!"

"Yeah." I nodded. "It's a lot more fun being here than being at my house. So what are you doing, teaching?"

"Helping." Arien's eyes carefully followed the kids even as she talked to me. "If I were paid for this, I'd lose my amateur standing. So Coach Davison's the official coach, and Tommy and I help out on Tuesdays and Thursdays. When the kids leave, we have the rink to ourselves for more practice."

Brittany came clip-clipping by, taking little baby steps, but smiling up at Arien. "Way to go, Brittany!" Arien encouraged her. "Keep it up!"

"She's darling," I said. "I didn't know they made skating skirts that small."

"They do," Arien said. "I wish I had started when I was that small." She looked over at the red-haired girl. "Tuck it in, Taryn!" she yelled, then she looked back at me. "I'll talk to you when I have a break, Cass. Duty calls."

I nodded, and she pushed off and was across the rink before I could bat an eye.

I was halfway through my geometry when a whistle blew and the little kids all skated off the rink and headed for home. I checked my watch—five o'clock.

Arien skated over to my table, but Tommy went straight for the snack bar. Honestly, for a kid I had known since kindergarten, he sure kept to himself. You'd think he'd at least acknowledge my presence!

Coach Davison came out of the office, a clipboard in his hand. He nodded at me, then looked at Arien. "Aren't you going to introduce us?" he asked pleasantly.

"This is Cassie Perkins, a friend from school," Arien explained. "She's a musician. Cassie, this is Coach Terry Davison."

I blushed but shook Coach Davison's hand when he offered it. "It's good to know you. Maybe you can help us select a song for these routines. Most of the usual music is just a tad short of awful." The coach motioned for Tommy to join us and he did, sitting as far away as he could without being in the next booth.

"Why do they use awful music for skating?" I asked, remembering the organ music I'd heard the day before. "There are so many good songs you could use."

"Well, skaters have to choose music that will please the judges," Coach Davison explained. "And even though most skaters are young, most judges are old. You can't skate to Madonna and expect the judges to like your music."

Arien laughed, and even Tommy smiled.

"But why can't you use music with lyrics?" I asked. "I mean, there are so many beautiful songs with words."

Coach Davison smiled. "Some people say that requiring music without vocals makes a clear distinction between amateur competitions and professional shows. But I think the purpose of skating competition is to see how well a skater interprets rhythms. If you added words, the skater might try to interpret the lyrics, and we'd have a fine mess."

"It's like ballet," Arien said. "Ballet dancers don't need vocal music to tell a story. They tell a story through interpretations of the rhythms."

"The long program also has to have several tempo

changes," Tommy added. It was the first time I think I'd ever heard Tommy say anything of his own free will, and my surprise must have shown on my face. He looked down awkwardly. "I mean, in the free-style competition, you have to show different kinds of techniques, so you need different styles and tempos."

"Which reminds me," Arien said, reaching over to tug on Tommy's sleeve. "Why aren't you going to try for the freestyle competition this year? You could win it, you know. You know all the moves."

Tommy just looked down at the ice left in his cup, and Coach Davison looked at Arien and shook his head. "It's no use," he said. "I've tried to talk him into it, but he just insists on doing figures and the pairs skating with you."

While the coach went on to discuss the details of a dance routine with Arien, I thought about Tommy. What was it that made him so solitary? Was he so shy that he couldn't and wouldn't even compete alone? He did the figures alone, true, but they were very disciplined and very routine. A skater either did them well, or he didn't. There wasn't much room for criticism unless a skater really messed up.

Arien brought me back with a question: "Cassie, you know music. What's a good song for my freestyle routine? I want something fresh and familiar that the audience will enjoy."

"I don't know." I was stumped. "I can't think of anything without lyrics."

"We could use a song with words, but it's got to be something that will still sound good when we take the voices out."

"Take the voices out? How do you do that?"

Coach Davison answered. "We do it with a vocal eliminator. It removes the recording track where the voices were recorded, but unfortunately, sometimes it also takes out the melody. All that's left is mush."

My mind was still blank. "I don't know," I answered. "But I'll go through my records tonight and see if I can come up with something, OK? I'll let you know tomorrow."

"OK." Arien smiled. "There's an invitational competition next month in Pensacola, so I've got to nail things down now." Her eyes twinkled. "Want to come?"

Did I! "Sure," I gulped. "Could I?"

Arien nodded. "It's over a weekend, so you won't even have to miss school. We'll leave on Friday and be back by Sunday night. Coach Davison, Tommy, me, and my mother are going. There's room for you if you want to come."

I felt my heart pounding. "I wouldn't miss it."

8

The next afternoon I had Max with me at the rink. I had no choice. It was our weekend with Dad, and Dad didn't want to make two trips to pick us up, so if I went to the rink, I had to take Max along. Dad said he'd pick us both up when he got off work.

At least Max didn't complain about the situation. As usual, he was curious about seeing something new, and I knew he'd enjoy seeing Arien and Tommy skate.

Arien waved when we came in, but Coach Davison was talking to her out on the rink, so she didn't come over. Tommy actually looked over at us. He didn't wave or even nod, but at least he wasn't ignoring me like he usually did. *I'll never understand him*, I thought with a shake of my head.

I climbed up on the table in the snack bar and watched, my chin in my hands. Max watched, too, for about five minutes, then he looked at me. "What do you think about Mom's baby?"

The question caught me by surprise. "What do

you mean, what do I think? I think it's stupid. Mom's too old to have a baby."

"No, she's not. I've been doing some research, and the oldest mother on record is Mrs. Ruth Kistler of Oregon. She had a healthy baby girl when she was fifty-seven. That's twenty years older than Mom."

"Good for Mrs. Kistler. Mom has two kids already—she doesn't need any more."

"The worldwide average is four children per mother," Max rattled on. "In Kenya, mothers bear an average of eight children."

"Good for the Kenyans. Max, do we really have to talk about this?"

"It's interesting. Did you know that right now, Mom's baby could easily fit into a chicken egg? And sometime in April, the baby will become conscious. We can shine a light on Mom's belly, and the baby will turn away."

I gave him my most disgusted look. "Max, that's gross. Mom's not about to let you shine a light on her belly."

Max held up a finger. "She just might. And by June the baby will learn to like music. Calm music will soothe him, and rock music will make the baby kick. Just think, in June the baby will even be able to smile."

"Not if you keep irritating him by playing music

and shining a light on him. What's with this 'him' business, anyway? It could be a girl, you know."

Max shrugged. "It could." He paused a moment, then said: "You don't want to talk about this, do you?"

"You're brilliant."

Max shut up for a while.

During the break, Arien skated over. "Hi," she said, breathless. "Did you find me a song?"

I nodded and pulled a record album out of my book bag. "This is one of my stepfather's records," I said, handing her the record. "It's the Los Angeles Philharmonic playing George Gershwin. How about 'Rhapsody in Blue'?"

Arien closed her eyes and thought. "I've heard of that. A lot of older people would know that, wouldn't they? It might just do. Let's play it and see how it skates."

She skated over to the sound booth and gave the record to Coach Davison. A few minutes later, the song came over the speakers and Arien began her routine.

Tommy, Coach Davison, Max, and I sat in the snack bar and watched quietly. Arien was incredible. Something in the song combined with her strength and power, and the routine came to life. When the music was slow and bluesy, Arien seemed flirtatious and coy. When the vibrant, rhythmic parts played, she came to life. The music seemed to call moves and gestures out of her soul, and everything came together perfectly.

"How long is it?" Coach Davison asked, checking the album. "Fifteen minutes and forty-five seconds? We'll have to cut it down, but that shouldn't be a problem."

As the music raged to its conclusion, Arien flew around the rink and ended with a spin on one leg that took my breath away. Her body was perfectly straight, parallel to the floor, and her face was toward the floor. Suddenly and smoothly, though, she turned herself up and over so that she was spinning straight and parallel again, but with her face up toward the ceiling.

"How'd she do that?" I gasped.

Coach Davison nodded. "Impressive, isn't it? She started out in a camel spin, then inverted it. Arien does that move better than anyone in competition today."

When she was finished, I burst out into applause, and Arien skated over to Coach Davison. "What did you think?" she asked, breathless. "I *love* it! It has everything we need."

Coach Davison nodded. "We'll have to cut it to five minutes," he said, "but there are enough variations that you should be able to get in all the compulsory jumps and spins. We'll give it a shot."

Arien sipped a glass of water with me and Max while Coach Davison worked with Tommy. "So this cute guy is your little brother?" she asked, smiling at Max. "I've seen him hanging out with Payton and the football players."

"He tutors them," I said simply. "He's a genius. Ask him anything, and he can give you an answer."

"OK." Arien crinkled her forehead in thought. "OK, Max, here's one for you. What's the meaning of life?"

I knew she was teasing, but Max took her seriously. "Actually, this is something I've been wanting to talk to Cassie about," he said. "Remember, Cass, a few months ago when you told me you believed in God?"

I nodded. Chip had told me that God loved me enough to send Jesus Christ to die for me, and I had given my life to God. It was all amazing to me, but I learned I could trust God even when my life was falling apart.

"Well, I asked you to prove God to me, but you said you couldn't. So I've been doing some thinking, and I think I've come up with the meaning of life."

"Call a press conference," Arien teased. "The whole world will want to know about this."

"I was thinking about Mom's baby," Max said.

Arien raised an eyebrow, and I nodded. "My mom's pregnant," I explained. "I'll tell you about it later."

Max went on. "I started wondering when the baby's life began. Was it when the egg became fertilized, or was it when the baby's heart began to beat?"

Arien leaned back and nodded. She was impressed.

"Then I realized," Max went on, "that life doesn't *begin* at all. I mean, the egg is alive before it is fertilized, because it's part of a living being, just like my foot is alive as long as it's a part of me. So life really doesn't *begin* when a baby's born, it's just passed on from one human being to another."

He paused for effect. "So I had to think: where did the first human life come from? I thought about the evolutionary model that says we descended from lower life forms, but that whole theory is hogwash because the scientific law of entropy says that all things gradually deteriorate, they don't *improve*."

"Can you get to the point, Max?" I interrupted. "You're losing me."

He nodded. "I looked in a Bible and read right there in the beginning that God breathed life into man after he had formed him from the dust of the ground. That makes sense. Our bodies are composed of the same elements as earth anyway, and it is much more logical to believe that God began life originally than to believe life evolved from mud and subatomic particles."

Arien's face was blank, and I was a little embarrassed. Not everyone knew how to take Max. She was probably bored to death.

"So that's the answer to your question," Max said, looking at Arien. "The meaning of life must be found in knowing *why* God gave life to us. We have to understand why we are here in the first place."

Arien leaned forward, and I realized I'd been wrong. She wasn't bored, she was intensely interested. "So why are we here?" she whispered.

Max looked at me. "Ask Cassie," he said simply. "I'd like to know myself."

I was flustered. I didn't know all the answers. I stammered: "Why don't you ask a preacher? All I know is that Chip said God loves us. We were supposed to be close to him, but God is holy and we're sinners. So Jesus, who didn't do anything wrong, was sent by God to pay for *our* sins by dying on the cross." I shrugged. "If you want to know God, you need to ask Jesus to take away your sins.

"Just ask him?" Max asked. "That's so simple."

I glared at him. "It would have to be for dummies like me to understand it," I snapped. "Not everything is complicated, Max."

"So if Jesus takes away our sin, then we can be with God, right?" Max thought aloud, his forehead crinkled in thought.

"We'll be with him when we die," I explained. "But for now, he hears our prayers and stays with us." I tried to remember how Chip explained it to me. "God—and Jesus—becomes your best friend."

Max nodded. "Well, if God made us so he could be our friend, then that's the meaning of life." He looked at Arien. "Got it?"

Coach Davison blew his whistle and Arien scooted out of the booth. "That makes sense," she said, gliding away. "I'm going to think about it."

Tommy came over then, pale and sweaty. He didn't go to the snack bar for his usual drink, instead he slumped in an empty booth and put his head on his arms. "He doesn't look so good," Max whispered. "Should we do something?"

I was about to walk over and check on Tommy, but Coach Davison skated around the corner. "I've called his folks," he explained. "I think Tommy's got a virus or something. We're going to let him go home and go to bed."

I backed away. The last thing I wanted was to get sick. Not when the world was finally beginning to look good.

9

March 1, Friday night, was circled in red on my calendar. I wasn't *really* serious when I asked Chip if he ever wanted to double with Arien and Payton. I had just wanted to see what Andrea would do. But on March 1, we *were* double-dating with them, and it hadn't even been my idea!

It had just been an ordinary afternoon at the rink when I had asked about some decorations Coach Davison was hanging on the rink walls. "It's the big free skate here on Friday night," Arien had explained during her practice break. "They're bringing in a disc jockey from WKIS and having a big skate. It's just for publicity, really, and the only charge will be for skate rental."

"Sounds like fun."

"It is." Arien's eyes had gotten a little misty. "My mom and dad met on skates, you know. Mom was at a skate with a short guy, and during 'Ladies' Choice' she went up to the tallest guy in the place and asked him to skate." She laughed. "The rest is history."

"My parents are divorced," I said abruptly. "It all happened last year. Now I've got a stepfather, and Mom's pregnant. I've also got a new stepbrother, and I only get to see Max on weekends." I paused a minute because I knew Arien's mom was in Florida and her dad was in California. "Are your parents separated?"

Arien shook her head. "No, not like that. Dad couldn't leave the farm—"

"A farm? With cows and horses and chickens?"

Arien laughed. "No. It's a vineyard. We live in the grape capital of the world. Anyway, since Mom and Dad wanted me to have the best coach they could find—" she shrugged, "here we are. But Mom and I will be here just for this year. After the nationals in July, we'll go back home. I'll probably go to college next year in California."

"What about Payton?"

Arien's cheeks turned slightly pink. "Well," she said, smiling, "we've talked about the future, and Payton's thinking about coming to California, too."

"Are you two *that* serious?"

Arien was watching Coach Davison hang decorations, and I wondered if she had heard me. But then she said, "Yes. I think we're that serious. I really think he's the guy for me."

I felt very immature. I was going to say something

about Chip, but she was talking about the guy she wanted to *marry*. Chip and I hadn't thought that far ahead.

"I wish I knew Payton better," I said, finally. "I'm sure he's great."

"Why don't you and Chip come to the skate Friday night?" Arien said, looking at me. "Payton and I will be here. Lots of kids will. Plus, it's a free skate, so it won't break Chip's budget."

I laughed. "OK, I'll ask him."

Tommy skated by then, on his way to get his afternoon Coke, and I broke the unwritten rule of our freshman class and spoke to him: "Hey, Tommy, are you coming to the skate Friday night?"

He whirled around on his skates, as surprised as I was that I'd spoken. "No," he muttered, still a little pale after being sick. "Why should I? All the kids at school hate me."

He whirled around again in one quick movement on his skates, and I thought about his answer. True, he was the resident geek of our class; he had been for years. We'd kind of gotten used to having him around, always quiet, always picked on or ignored. He was part of us though, one of our class. He'd always taken Eric Brandt's bullying so quietly that we thought he just didn't care. I never dreamed he thought we hated him—it was just that no one *liked* him.

"You ought to come," I called loudly as he skated behind the snack bar. "You're a better skater than anyone in our class."

He didn't look up, but I could see him shake his head as he filled a paper cup with ice. "It doesn't matter," he said quietly. Then he poured his drink and took it over to a far booth where he sat down—alone, as usual.

Arien and I looked at each other. "I don't understand him," Arien said quietly so he wouldn't hear. "In the rink, he's great. Out of the rink, he seems so lonely. I think he needs to know that God loves him."

I looked at her in surprise, and she smiled. "Yeah," she continued. "I went home and thought about what you and Max had said. And I asked God to take my life and show me how to live it. There's still a lot I don't understand, but for the first time I feel like someone has an answer to my questions."

I didn't say anything. I couldn't do anything but grin like a Cheshire cat. Arien stood up and playfully pulled a strand of my hair. "So thanks, kiddo. I owe you a big one."

Practically everyone from Astronaut High was at Southland Roller Rink on Friday night. Melanie

Sergeant and her crowd were there, trying desperately to get a hulking football player to come out of the snack bar. The big lug wouldn't budge from his booth, afraid he'd fall on his rear. Andrea and Eric were there, holding hands and skating slowly even on the fast skates—I wasn't the only one who nearly tripped trying to get around them. Even Mr. Hinton, our principal, made an appearance and went around the rink a couple of times—he was pretty good on skates. Looking around, though, I saw no sign of Tommy McLaughlin.

Arien was different tonight. Her personality hadn't changed—she was still sweet and friendly to everyone—but her skating style was completely subdued. She must have realized that big and brawny Payton felt awkward on skates, because she skated quietly by his side, never once breaking out in anything flashy. She even sat out a lot when I knew she couldn't be tired. But she was happy, that was easy to see. Whenever Payton was around, her eyes glowed like candles shining in blue-green seawater.

Chip was a good skater—at least, he didn't fall down much—but he had absolutely no sense of rhythm. He did fine skating by himself, but whenever we tried to hold hands and skate, he'd miss the beat and send his foot crashing into mine, which nearly made me fall. I'm not a great skater either,

I'll be the first to admit, but at least I know when to move my feet with the music. After a few near falls, I told him to go on alone. I'd catch up with him later.

After about four songs, my legs felt shaky and I sat down. I don't know how Tommy and Arien managed to stand up after hours on skates. They had to have legs of iron, because even after twenty minutes mine felt like jelly.

Over in the sound booth, Coach Davison was playing the records while the WKIS disc jockey announced the songs. "Clear the floor," the deejay announced. "The next song is a trio skate. Trios only!"

Everyone scrambled to get either on or off the floor, and I saw Arien and Payton coming my way. "Come on," Arien called, grabbing my hand.

She swung me around to the far side, with Payton in between us, and I loved the song Coach Davison played: "That's What Friends Are For." We skated around and around, me flying out of control on the end, as we sang: "Keep smilin', keep shinin', knowing you can always count on me. . . ."

Once as we went around, I saw Andrea and Eric standing at the rail. Her eyes widened as she saw me go by with Arien and Payton, but instead of feeling smug, I felt kind of sorry. I didn't want to hurt Andrea, not really. I had been hurt myself.

When the trio skate was done, I turned to thank Arien and Payton, but I turned too quickly and fell flat on my rear. It was embarrassing, but I just laughed. "Help me up, will ya?" I held out one hand to Arien and tried to push myself up with the other. Arien's hand grabbed mine, but I was startled to feel how cold and clammy it was. I looked at her face, and something wasn't right. She was sweating so much her hair was wet around her forehead, and her eyes glittered against pale skin.

"You don't look so hot," I muttered.

"Is that all the thanks I get?" she teased. "After dragging you and Payton around the rink through two songs, I've got a right to work up a sweat."

But that wasn't it. She spoke in abrupt bursts, as if she were winded. I'd seen Arien skate for hours without seeming at all tired.

"You're sick, aren't you?" I asked.

"Just a little sore throat." She looked at Payton and laughed. "Nothing serious. But I didn't want to miss tonight."

"I'm taking you home," Payton offered gallantly. "I'll even tuck you in bed, if your mother will let me."

Arien leaned her head on Payton's shoulder, and they left the rink.

When it was time for the couples-only skate, I

found Chip at a pinball machine. "Come on," I said, pulling at his sleeve. "It's a couples skate."

Chip didn't take his hands off the pinball machine. "Go on, Cassie, I'm a klutz," he said, beating the flipper buttons furiously. "Let me pass on this one."

I clomped away unhappily. They were playing one of my favorite songs, but the skate was for couples only. Who else could I ask? Half the guys there were going with someone, so if I asked one of them, some girl would be furious with me. Worse yet, they might turn me down.

Behind me, I heard the door to the rink office slam. I turned and saw Tommy McLaughlin walk out, carrying his skates.

"Hurry up and put on those skates," I told him. "Hurry! This is my favorite song and it's couples only."

He looked at me as if I were crazy. "Hurry!" I yelled, and for some reason I still don't understand, he kicked off his shoes and put on his skates. We were on the floor in a minute flat.

I had never known that skating with a real skater could be so heavenly. Most of the couples on the floor were just skating while holding hands, but the pros did it the right way, with the guy skating backward and the girl's arms around his neck. Tommy whirled me around without thinking, and we skated together so effortlessly that I didn't even stop to think about *who* I was with. All I could think was that *this* was the way to skate. He must have had eyes in the back of his head because even skating backward, he easily pulled me through the crowds of struggling couples without missing a pulse of the music.

The music stopped, but the Couples Only sign stayed lit, so we kept skating while we waited for the next song. The only sound was the whoosh of our skates in an easy rhythm, and in the quiet, I felt a little awkward. Tommy probably thought I was crazy, or that I had a crush on him or something. I looked up at him, though, and he wasn't even looking at me. He was staring off over my head.

A new song started, and I forgot to worry about what people were thinking. I wasn't good, but with Tommy guiding me, leaning into the curves on the rink and with the flow of the music, I felt graceful and accomplished. Best of all, I knew that if I stumbled or slipped, Tommy would catch me.

Since Tommy wouldn't look at me, I looked away at the faces of the kids lining the rails. A couple of people had their mouths open and as I passed Leah Stiles I heard her yell, "Cassie! What are you doing?"

Holly Musgrave yelled, "Way to go, Cassie!" and I

wasn't sure what she meant. When we passed
Andrea I heard her yell, "What will Chip say?" but I
didn't care. He was the one who didn't want to skate.

When the music stopped again and the All Skate
sign flashed, Tommy took his hands from around
my waist and I lowered mine from his neck. "OK?"
he asked, looking down at me for the first time.
"Will you leave me alone now?"

I nodded, and he skated off the rink and over to
the side. I knew he would disappear again, off into
the night. People who hadn't actually seen us skating would never believe it had happened.

The news traveled fast, though, because as I made
my way around the outside of the rink, I saw Chip
coming toward me. "Want something to eat?" he
yelled above the noise.

I nodded, and when I finally reached him through
the crowd, he held out his hand and we clump-
clumped our way to a booth at the snack bar. Before
skating off to place our order, though, Chip leaned
down. "You'll never believe what I heard," he said,
grinning.

"What?"

"I heard you were skating with another guy, and
for a minute I was actually jealous."

"You were?" I pretended to be surprised.

"Yeah, but then I heard who you were skating with, so I knew there was nothing to worry about."

Chip rolled off, as confident as ever. I was pleased that he was jealous but a little bothered that he didn't see Tommy as a threat. Couldn't anyone else see that Tommy McLaughlin wasn't a total misfit?

10

Mom and Tom were a little reluctant to let me go to Pensacola for the skating invitational. One night I slipped downstairs to the kitchen for a glass of milk and heard them in the library. "Why does she want to go?" Tom asked, sounding exasperated. "She doesn't even skate, does she? It just doesn't make sense."

"She's found a new friend," Mom explained. "Besides, Tom, I think it's giving her something to think about besides the changes in her own life. This hasn't been an easy time for Cassie, you know."

"Nick's handled it well," Tom countered. "Max seems to be fine. Why should Cassie be upset?"

"Cassie's different," Mom murmured. "She feels things deeply, and I think this baby has really upset her."

I didn't want to hear anymore, so I quietly closed the refrigerator door and slipped back up the stairs to my room. Maybe it didn't make sense to them, but I knew that Arien's friendship had kept me going these last two months. I couldn't help but think that God had brought her into my life, and somehow we were supposed to help each other.

On March 16, I met Arien, her mother, Coach Davison, and Tommy at the rink after school. "Are you ready?" Arien asked, her eyes glowing with excitement.

Mrs. Belle wasn't at all what I expected. I thought Arien's mother would be tall and elegant, but Mrs. Belle looked just like anyone else's mother. She was brunette, with more than a few gray hairs sprinkled in her bangs, and was totally motherly looking.

Coach Davison and Tommy rode up front in Coach Davison's car, and we girls rode in back. "Now what's this invitational competition all about?" I asked, determined to know everything I could.

"For one thing, it's giving us a chance to practice our routines and dances before the regional in June," Arien explained. "Not to mention the chance it gives us to look at our competition. If the other routines are harder than mine, I'll have to make mine a lot tougher."

"It's a good practice run," Coach Davison explained from the front seat. "The results don't count in the official competition, but we'd be nuts to turn down the opportunity."

Arien leaned toward the front seat. "Did you get the practice schedule?" she asked. "When can we practice?"

Coach Davison laughed. "The competition starts at ten o'clock," he said. "And your practice slot is from five to six tomorrow morning."

Arien fell back with a mock groan.

"Five *in the morning?*" I asked, horrified.

Arien nodded. "At least we have a chance to practice." She elbowed me. "I hope you didn't plan on getting much sleep."

"You girls may not have planned on sleeping, but I did," interrupted Mrs. Belle. She tried to put her hand across Arien's forehead, but Arien ducked.

"I'm fine, Mom," she sighed. "Just fine."

"I don't know, honey," Mrs. Belle answered. "Coach, did you know Arien's lost ten pounds in the last two months? Her skating outfit just hangs on her."

"She'll be lighter when we do the lifts," Tommy joked. "That helps me out a lot."

I saw Coach's eyes in the rearview mirror. He was studying Arien carefully. "You've been working very hard, Arien," he said slowly. "You are eating, aren't you?"

"I'm not anorexic, if that's what you're getting at," Arien laughed. "I've just been nervous, that's all.

97

Excited. Plus, I had that sore throat a couple of weeks ago—I guess I just haven't had an appetite. But just wait until this invitational is over. Next week I'll be eating like a horse."

"Great," Tommy groaned. "I'll never be able to lift you."

The next morning, our alarm clock buzzed at four-thirty. A minute later, a sleepy desk clerk rang our room. "This is your wake-up call," he said.

"Thanks," I heard Arien mutter. "We're up."

I sat up, shaking my head and trying to wake up.

"You don't have to get up," Arien whispered, trying not to wake her mother. "You can sleep if you want to."

"No way," I whispered back. "I want to be in on all of this."

We pulled on our sweatsuits in the semidarkness and slipped out of the motel room. Tommy and Coach Davison were waiting by the car.

"Good morning," Coach Davison's voice boomed. "Did you sleep well?"

"Was that sleep?" Arien joked. "It felt more like a catnap. I don't feel so hot."

"You're just not awake yet," Coach Davison said, unlocking the car. "Come on, gang. I'll get us four cups of coffee while you guys warm up. You'll be awake in no time."

The empty skating rink felt strange. It was silent except for the whir of Arien's and Tommy's skates, and under the lights, I thought Arien looked a little green. After skating for about thirty minutes, she came over to the edge of the rink and collapsed, shivering.

She buried her head in her arms and called out in a muffled voice: "Tommy?"

"What?" He was standing a few feet away, his usual blank look in place.

"Remember when you had that virus? What did it feel like?"

Tommy closed his eyes. "Stomach cramps, fever, diarrhea, vomiting, and muscle aches."

"Oh no." Arien moaned.

Coach Davison leaned over her. "Do you think you're sick?"

Arien's head moved. "Yes," she whispered.

"Come on, then." Coach Davison looked up. "Tommy, you keep practicing your figures. I'm going to take Arien to her mother, let her sleep, give her aspirin and chicken soup. The pairs competition isn't until after lunch, so maybe she'll be better by then. OK?"

Tommy nodded slowly and skated out to the circles to practice. Coach Davison looked at me. "Cassie, I need your help. Arien and Tommy are both entered in figures, which starts at ten. Arien will drop out, but you've got to be here for Tommy at ten. Do you mind staying here with him?"

I didn't want to stay in an empty skating rink all morning with Tommy McLaughlin, but what could I do? It was an emergency. I nodded.

"OK. Here are the papers you'll need. Take them to the judges at about nine-thirty and explain that Arien is dropping out of the figures. But she and Tommy will still be competing as a dance team, and Arien will also compete in freestyle tomorrow. Got it?"

I nodded. As Coach Davison practically carried Arien away, I bowed my head and muttered probably the most sincere prayer I'd ever prayed: "God, please strengthen Arien. She's worked hard, and she deserves a chance. Please, God, help her."

I sat down to watch Tommy skate in circles.

At one o'clock, I saw Coach Davison and Arien enter the rink. Arien looked beautiful, if a little pale. She was wearing a stunning aqua skating outfit spangled with sequins. Her blonde hair was pulled back tightly, and glitter sparkled through it.

Coach Davison found her a seat and ran to where I was sitting. "Is everything all set?" he asked.

"Everything's fine," I said. "Tommy won a silver medal in the figures. I wish you could have seen it."

Coach Davison nodded, pleased. "I knew he could do it. Where is he?"

"Eating lunch," I said. "He'll be back any minute."

Coach Davison walked over to the registration table, and I went to Arien. She was huddled under a jacket even though the building was warm. "Hi," she whispered, looking up at me. "Can you believe this? I just hope you don't get sick."

"Don't worry, I take vitamins," I joked, sitting down next to her. I put my hand on her forehead, careful not to smudge her makeup. "Good grief, you're burning up."

"I know." She gritted her teeth and tried to smile. "But I think I can forget about it for at least a few minutes."

I nodded. "Once I had this audition and woke up that morning with a fever and a sore throat," I said. "I went to school anyway, sick as a dog, but determined to audition anyway. They called my number, I sang my heart out, and went home to bed."

Arien's teeth were chattering. "Did you get the part?"

I nodded. "Yep. The starring role. So if I could do it, you can do this."

Tommy came over then, and I was surprised because he looked like a different person. He was wearing a one-piece tuxedo suit with a waist-cut jacket that made him look even taller and more trim. He was positively handsome, and his red hair looked striking. He didn't look a thing like Bozo now.

"Hi," he said to Arien. "Are you going to make it?"

"You bet." Arien smiled at him. He took her hand almost tenderly and held it. "OK, let's do it," he said, then he knelt at her feet and put her skates on her feet.

He had just slipped the boot cover over her skates when Coach Davison rushed over. "You're next," he said, helping Arien to her feet.

"OK." She tossed her head back, clenched her teeth into a smile, and tossed the jacket on her shoulders to me. "Let's do it, partner," she said to Tommy, and hand in hand, they skated out onto the rink and got into position.

I walked over to the rail, thinking that I'd never seen anything more brave. They smiled at the audience, the music began, and off they went.

They skated throughout the afternoon—two dances in the elimination rounds, then, after they had advanced, two dances in the finals. When they were finally announced as first-place winners, they skated together out to the winner's podium where a little girl placed a bouquet in Arien's arms and Tommy was handed a golden trophy.

Coming out of the rink, though, Arien collapsed

in her mother's arms. Tommy picked her up and carried her to the car, and we took her back to the motel and put her to bed.

The next morning Arien was no better. She was worse, in fact. "There's no way she can compete in freestyle today," Coach Davison said. "We'll withdraw and take her home. Maybe it's for the best. She'll be our secret weapon in the regional."

Mrs. Belle nodded, but she looked worried. She put her hand on Arien's forehead again. "Poor thing," she said, "skating her heart out yesterday and not even able to sit up today."

"It's just a virus," Tommy muttered from the doorway. "She'll be fine next week."

We packed our suitcases and went home. Arien wasn't in school on Monday, and when I called her house, her mother said they'd spent the day at the doctor's office. They thought it was a virus, but they were running tests to make sure.

After Arien missed an entire week of school, I rode my bike to the apartment complex where she and her mother lived. When Mrs. Belle opened the door, I smiled. "Since Arien's trying to skip as much school as possible, I thought I'd come lecture her," I teased.

Mrs. Belle burst into tears.

"What's wrong?" I asked, embarrassed. Had I said the wrong thing?

"The doctors wanted to know how long she had been sick," Mrs. Belle said, wiping her eyes. "And they asked why she was so thin."

"She doesn't have that disease where you don't eat," I said firmly. "I've seen her eat."

Mrs. Belle shook her head. "No. But she has swollen glands, and she's been having fevers and not telling us about them. She's been sick for two months, Cassie—"

"She's had the flu," I interrupted. "Tommy had a virus or something, and there's something going around school. She'll be OK."

Mrs. Belle shook her head and her eyes filled with tears. For a minute she couldn't speak at all, then she cleared her throat. "They asked if she had ever used drugs," she whispered hoarsely, "and when she said yes, they said they wanted to do more tests."

"That was a long time ago," I cried out. "She's not a junkie or anything."

"No, she's not a junkie," Mrs. Belle's voice softened. "She has a virus, Cassie, but it's not just any virus. It's HIV."

I had to stop and think. What was the HIV virus, and why was Mrs. Belle so upset?

"HIV?" I wondered aloud. "Isn't that the virus that causes—"

"AIDS," Mrs. Belle whispered, leaning against the door frame. "It causes AIDS."

11

"Barbara, you shouldn't have said that." I heard a man's voice, and soon he stepped into view. "Why don't you come in?" he asked politely. "I'm Leland Belle, Arien's father."

Mr. and Mrs. Belle stepped back, and I hesitantly went into the living room and sat in a chair near the door. I didn't know what to say. Most of all, I was scared to touch anything. If Arien had AIDS, weren't we all in danger? My mind was racing with thoughts of the times I'd shared a Coke with her—the times she and Tommy positioned their heads within inches of each other while they were skating—the strange virus Tommy had a few weeks ago. Good grief, what if we all had the AIDS virus?

Mrs. Belle sat timidly on the couch and wiped her eyes with the handkerchief her husband handed her. "I'm sorry, Leland's right," she said, her voice quavering. "I shouldn't have said anything, but sometimes I think I'll scream if I can't say something." Her chin quivered and she looked down at the rug. "I'm just so upset, I'm not thinking clearly."

Mr. Belle gave me a stern look. "Young lady, I understand that you're a friend of Arien's. If you're really her friend, you'll keep this information to yourself. Just because Arien has the HIV virus, it doesn't mean that you or anyone else at school can catch the virus from her. If this got out . . ." He paused. "Well, I don't have to tell you what hysterical people can do. Arien has only a few months of school left, and there are only a few months left in this skating season. Please don't mess things up for her."

He was scolding me, and I hadn't even done anything. "I won't say anything," I whispered, "but I don't understand. How did Arien get this?"

Mr. and Mrs. Belle looked at each other. "We don't know for sure, but we're going to investigate," Mr. Belle said. "We know she didn't get it from anyone here in Florida. The doctors say she's probably been carrying the virus for at least four years."

I had to let it all sink in. Four years? That meant Arien got the HIV virus when she was my age—fourteen, or maybe even thirteen.

I looked down at my hands. "Where is she?" I asked.

"She's in the hospital for now, but she's better and

she'll be coming home soon," her father said smoothly. "Then she'll be going back to school, I'll go back out to California, and she'll start skating again. We want her life to be as normal as possible."

"I know she'd appreciate it if you called her," Mrs. Belle said, smiling crookedly. "And she wanted me to ask you to pray for her."

I nodded. "OK." I stood up and unconsciously wiped my hands on my jeans. "It was nice to meet you." I nodded to Mr. Belle, then I practically ran out the door. I couldn't wait to get out of there.

The first person I called was Max. "Max," I whispered on the phone, "I need some information. Serious information, and I can't tell you why I need it. You can't ask, either, and you can't tell anyone about this."

Max was curious. "Sure, Cass. What do you need?"

"I need information on AIDS and the HIV virus."

"Wow." Max was impressed. "I take it this *isn't* for a school paper?"

Why hadn't I thought of that excuse? "No, it's not," I whispered. "I just need it, OK?"

"OK," Max said. "I'll use Dad's computer and tap into my research database tonight. I'll get back to you."

I couldn't call Arien. I didn't know what to say. All I knew about AIDS was that there was no cure and people died from it. I knew that most people who got it were either drug users or homosexuals, and I knew Arien wasn't either one of those. But if she had it, she would die from it, and what could I say to her?

I did pray for her. A lot. I wondered if it was a waste of time because what could God do for someone with AIDS other than work an out-and-out miracle and heal them? So I prayed at first that it was all a terrible mistake. Maybe she had mono or hepatitis or Asian flu or something. All-American homecoming queens just didn't get AIDS.

I wanted to talk to Chip about it because he knew so much more about God than I did. But I had promised to keep this news a secret, and even if I hinted around he'd be sure to guess who I was talking about. So I knew I couldn't talk about AIDS.

I went to church on Wednesday night with Chip. Doug Richlett, our youth pastor, was having a "Brain Brawl" night where we asked questions about anything, and he gave us answers from the Bible.

The other kids mostly asked questions about dating, movies, and music. It all sounded pretty stupid compared to what I had been thinking about. When I had a chance, I raised my hand.

"Cassie?" Doug asked. "What's your question?"

"What happens to Christians when they die?" I

asked. "And why do some people die young and others live to be a hundred? Is that fair?"

"Those are good questions," Doug said. Chip gave me a curious look, but I just kept looking at Doug. "As humans, we tend to live in the here and now and we forget that in God's eyes, time does not exist. So we think that a human life of, say, twenty years is very short. But in God's perspective, a human life of even a hundred years is just a short breath of life."

Doug opened his Bible. "No matter how long we live, we know we don't have to fear death. In Psalm 116:15 the Bible says: 'Precious in the sight of the Lord is the death of his saints.' When a Christian dies, he or she goes to be with the Lord. It's like a grand homecoming, and the Lord rejoices when his child finally comes home. It's a day of victory, not defeat."

I sat quietly, thinking, and someone else asked another question. Chip leaned toward me and whispered: "Is someone in your family sick?"

I frowned. "No. I was just wondering."

Chip looked ahead and nodded. "Oh."

Arien was back in school on Thursday. I saw her in a group of senior girls before school started, and I heard part of their conversation. "Pneumonia?" Linda Peterson asked. "How awful!"

Arien covered her mouth and coughed. "I'm better now, though."

I tried to slip past in the crowd, but Arien saw me.

"Cassie!" she called, smiling.

"Hi," I called back. "I'll catch you later, OK? I've got to meet Chip."

It was sort of the truth, I would meet Chip in first period. But the real truth was that I felt awkward to be around Arien, plus I was scared stiff about catching AIDS from her. She didn't look sick, but she hadn't looked sick before, either, and the doctors said she'd been carrying the virus for years. I didn't want to get it.

Just after the bell rang, an announcement came over the intercom: a special assembly had been called in the auditorium. We were dismissed immediately.

Miss Chamberlain looked as surprised as we were, so we all gathered our books and left.

Our principal, Mr. Hinton, stood on the stage, and the crowd finally got quiet. With him were a lady in a navy blue pants and a light blue top, and a slim man in tweed pants and a sweater. The sweater was strange—it was warm outside.

Mr. Hinton introduced the lady as Mrs. Fleming, an official with the public health department. "Mrs. Fleming is here to talk to you about AIDS and the

HIV virus," Mr. Hinton said. "I want you to pay special attention to this information. I'll let her introduce her guest."

Max was sitting three rows down in front, and I saw him turn to look at me. I gave him a warning look.

Mrs. Fleming smiled. "First of all, you should understand that AIDS stands for Acquired Immune Deficiency Syndrome. It is a condition where the body's immune systems fail. It is caused by a virus we call HIV," she said. "A person with HIV does *not* necessarily have AIDS. Sometimes a person with HIV can go as long as eight years without ever showing signs of AIDS."

There was a flurry of movement down at the end of my row. Obviously some kids were goofing off because they thought this wasn't important—that AIDS could never happen to them. I knew better.

Mrs. Fleming knew how to get their attention. "I'd like to introduce my guest, Miles Zug," she said. "Please give him your full attention."

Miles Zug stood up and looked us over. He was about thirty and good-looking, with a nice beard and shiny brown hair. He seemed confident and even more self-assured than Mr. Hinton. He was either a salesman or a professor, I decided. No one else could get up in my school and not feel at least a little bit nervous.

"I'm thirty-two, married, and I have two kids," Mr. Zug began. "I'm pleased to meet each of you, because now that you know me, you can't say you don't know anyone with AIDS."

The miscellaneous shuffling stopped. I closed my eyes, not even wanting to look at Mr. Miles Zug. I didn't want to know two people with AIDS.

"When I found out I had the HIV virus, it was like being hit by a truck going fifty miles an hour," Mr. Zug went on. "Since that day I've had pneumonia five times, I have high fevers off and on, and the doctors have tried all kinds of drugs on me. I'm beginning to feel like I've tangled with a porcupine, I've been stuck so many times."

Some kid in front snickered, and Mr. Zug looked down at him for a minute before going on. "I'm here today to try to save your lives," he said. "It doesn't matter how I got AIDS, what matters is what you can do to make sure you don't get it. Mrs. Fleming will give you some guidelines, and if you're smart, you'll listen."

Too late, I thought. *For one of us, you're at least four years too late.*

Mrs. Fleming stood up. "You can't get the HIV virus through shaking hands, a kiss on the cheek, or through sharing food with someone who has the virus," she said. "You can't get the HIV virus through a sneeze, a cough, mosquitoes, pets, donating blood, swimming pools, drinking fountains, toilet seats, or doorknobs."

She smiled at us. "Who knows how you *can* get the HIV virus?"

I knew. A lot of people knew, but there was no way we were going to raise our hands. But, amazingly, Tommy McLaughlin's hand shot up.

"Yes, young man?" Mrs. Fleming nodded at Tommy. "How is the virus passed?"

"Through homosexuals," Tommy said. The group of kids around Eric Brandt erupted in laughter.

"Homosexuals are a high risk group," Mrs. Fleming said, her eyes serious. "But it's not just homosexuals who can pass the AIDS virus. The point is, you have to *do* something to get AIDS. And to keep from getting AIDS, you have to say no to certain behaviors."

"Listen carefully," Mr. Zug interjected.

"First of all, don't do drugs," she said. "Never share a needle with anyone. In New York City, it is estimated that 50 percent of all IV drug users may be infected with the HIV virus. So stay away from drugs!"

She looked us over carefully. "Next, remember it's

more than OK to say no to sex. Not having sexual intercourse is the only sure way to avoid infection by the AIDS virus through sex. If you sleep with one person, you are sleeping with everyone he or she has ever had sexual relations with. People can pass the AIDS virus without realizing they ever had it."

I sneaked a look over where the seniors were sitting. Arien was sitting between Melanie Sergeant and Payton. Payton was laughing with the guy on the other side of him, but Arien was sitting quietly with her head down.

I couldn't help but wonder—how serious had Arien and Payton been? Was it possible that Payton had the virus, too? If it was, would Arien tell him?

12

"Are there any questions?"

A few hands shot up, and I leaned forward, trying to hear every word.

"What if you think you might have AIDS?"

"The Public Health Service National AIDS Hotline is 1-800-342-AIDS." She paused while a few people grabbed pencils to write down the number.

"Can you get AIDS from French-kissing?"

Mrs. Fleming hesitated. "Doctors have not found anyone who got AIDS from French-kissing," she said. "But the AIDS virus is found in all body fluids, including tears and saliva. The U.S. Public Health Service does say that people who have the HIV virus should avoid open-mouthed kissing."

"Is it safe to go to school with someone who has AIDS?"

Mrs. Fleming nodded. "Yes, as long as the person hasn't developed another contagious infection like chicken pox or tuberculosis. Of course, if you had chicken pox or TB, you'd stay home anyway until you were better."

Melanie Sergeant raised her hand. "If someone at school had AIDS, they'd tell us, right? I mean, we can't be expected to go to school with someone who's got it."

Mrs. Fleming didn't even pause, but I saw Mr. Hinton shift his weight uncomfortably. "Actually, as long as the person remains well, there is no reason to give out that information," Mrs. Fleming said firmly. "Only the person's doctor, the school superintendent, and a public health official need to know."

Melanie stood up defiantly. "Does someone at this school have AIDS? Is that why you're here?"

Mr. Hinton stepped between the microphone and Mrs. Fleming. "Sit down, Miss Sergeant," he said flatly. "You've already asked your question."

Mrs. Fleming stepped back up to the microphone. "I'm here because you need this information," she said smoothly. "Over the last two years the number of HIV-infected teenagers has increased by 40 percent. You *must* listen. This information can save your life."

Melanie sat down abruptly, then leaned toward her friends and the group buzzed angrily. I closed my eyes tightly, fearing the worst. Did Melanie suspect something, or was she just making trouble as usual?

When I got home, I was surprised to see Mom in her first maternity smock. With all that had been going on, I'd almost been able to forget that she was pregnant. I wanted to forget it, but from now on it would be nearly impossible.

"I know, I'm getting fat," Mom said when she caught me looking at her belly. "Don't you dare give me a hard time."

"I won't." I put my books on the table in the foyer and started toward the kitchen for my after-school Coke.

"By the way, Cass," Mom said, following me, "is your friend Arien any better? You haven't been to the skating rink in a couple of weeks now."

"She's better," I said, taking a glass from the cupboard. "I just haven't been in the mood to go down there, that's all."

"I see." Mom gave me one of those I-can-see-you-don't-want-to-talk-about-it looks.

I filled my glass with ice from the freezer and grabbed a can of Coke from the fridge. "It's Max's weekend here, right?" I asked.

"Yes," Mom said, nodding. "Do you two have something special planned?"

"I just want to talk to him, that's all," I said,

gathering my glass, Coke, and books from the hall. "I'll be in my room. I have a lot of homework."

Arien called me that night. "Hi, Cass," she said, sounding like her old self. "How've you been?"

"Fine," I said. "How are you?"

"OK," she said. She waited a minute, then added, "Mom told me she told you."

"Yeah."

"I'm glad, you know. It may sound crazy, but I know I can trust you not to blab it all over school. And it helps to have at least one person to talk to. My mom can't talk about it, and my dad had to go back to California."

Brother, I thought. *Doesn't she know I can't talk about it either? It gives me the creeps.*

I finally said, "So how are you *really* doing?"

"Good," Arien said. "I had a kind of pneumonia because my immune system has been weakened. But my fever's down, and I'll be fine, for a while at least."

She paused, expecting me to say something. "That's good," I said. Then, although it was none of my business, I had to ask: "Does Payton know?"

"No," she said. "There's no reason for him to know." When I didn't answer, she put it more bluntly: "We never went all the way, Cassie. We thought it would complicate things. Now I'm really glad we didn't."

I was glad she couldn't see my face. I was too embarrassed.

"I'm starting training again next week," she said brightly. "Tommy and I only have ten weeks until the regional competition in July. I'm just not going to think about *anything* but winning that gold medal. I'd love for you to come to the rink again, if you want."

"I don't know," I hedged. I didn't want to promise anything. "I've been working on some new songs for my voice lessons, and Mom's finally beginning to look pregnant. We'll probably have to do some shopping or something for the baby. Maybe we'll wallpaper the nursery next week."

Arien took the hint. "I see. OK, I guess I'll see you whenever."

"OK." Boy, was this awkward. "I've been praying for you."

"Really? Thanks." She hung up. I put down the phone, put my head in my pillow, and cried.

When Dad dropped Max at our house on Friday night, I waited until Max had brought his stuff in, then I cornered him in the library. "OK," I whispered. "I know all the stuff the school nurse said. Now what else can you tell me about AIDS?"

"I don't know what else you want to know," Max said. "But I can tell you AIDS is a serious threat to kids. Although less than six hundred kids between thirteen and nineteen have AIDS, the number infected with HIV is possibly a hundred times higher. Another study of teenagers showed that 70 percent were sexually active, but only 15 percent said they changed their behavior because of the threat of AIDS."

"Wow." I sat down on the couch, unable to believe that only 15 percent of those kids took AIDS seriously.

"That's not the worst of it," Max said seriously. "Of those 15 percent who changed their behavior, only 20 percent of them were using effective methods of preventing AIDS." Max shrugged. "Most kids just think AIDS is something that could never happen to them."

I bit my lip. I wanted to say, "Oh, yes it can happen; it has happened to someone really close to us," but I just muttered, "Anything else?"

"Just a couple more things. First, kids who experiment early with smoking, sex, or drugs are in danger. Girls who look more mature than their age are at risk—you know," he said, "like Arien Belle."

I gasped. Did Max know?

He did now. He saw my expression and his mouth opened.

"You don't mean—"

"I'm not saying anything, Max. I promised. Go on."

Max sank on the couch next to me and stared at the wall of books. "Once the virus develops into full-blown AIDS and begins to weaken the immune system, the average survival time is eighteen months," he said simply. "Usually by then the patient has contracted a disease the weakened immune system can't fight off. When your immune system is weak, there are lots of diseases that can be life-threatening."

I was ready to cry, and Max actually held my hand. His brown eyes were serious. "Who knows? If a person is young and physically fit, maybe it will take longer."

We sat on the couch together, staring at Tom's endless rows of books. Finally Max asked, "What are you going to do?"

"I don't know," I whispered. "I just don't know."

13

I didn't tell, I promise I didn't tell. Max guessed, but he didn't tell anyone either. But somehow the news got out. I heard that Melanie Sergeant started it all.

After that little scene in the school auditorium, Melanie got it in her head that someone in our school had AIDS. So she started snooping. She and her friends sat around trying to figure out who'd been absent a lot in the last month, and the first person they thought of was Arien Belle.

We freshmen don't eat lunch with the upper-classmen, but Holly Musgrave heard all about it from her older sister, and Holly told me what happened. It seems that Arien walked over to the table where she and Melanie usually ate, and Melanie and all the other girls were there. Melanie looked up at Arien and said, "So what was wrong with you last week, anyway? What exactly did the doctor say?"

Arien had shrugged and said, "If you really want to know Mel, I was throwing up and had a fever. I really don't think you want to hear about it at lunch."

Melanie got louder. "What caused it? And I heard you were in the hospital—they don't put you in a hospital for flu, Arien."

"They do if it's pneumonia," Arien said, calmly sitting her tray down on the table. "Anyway, I feel fine. Let's eat."

"But why did the health department send a nurse the day you came back to school?" Melanie persisted, practically screaming. Every eye in the lunchroom was watching that table.

"I'm sure it was just a coincidence," Arien said, sitting down. "Will you hush so we can eat?"

"I think you've got AIDS," Melanie shrieked. "If you think I'm staying at this table, you're crazy."

At this point, Arien's face went pale, but everyone could tell she was furious. "I don't care what you do," she said sharply. "But I do have the HIV virus. And you can't get it from me. So sit down or leave, Melanie, but shut up."

Holly's sister said that up until then, Melanie was probably just trying to give Arien a hard time. Everyone knows that Melanie's jealous of Arien, even though she pretends to be her best friend. They all thought Melanie's little scene was just an attempt to make trouble for Arien. But when Arien admitted

126

she had the AIDS virus the whole cafeteria became totally, deathly silent.

Melanie stood up, picked up her tray, and dumped it in the garbage can. The other girls looked at Arien, then at Melanie. Then they got up, too, and dumped their trays. No one wanted to eat food that Arien had even passed by.

The news spread like wildfire through the cafeteria, and it didn't take more than sixty seconds for Payton and his football friends to hear it out on the patio where they ate. I heard the story in detail—at first he laughed and said they were crazy; Arien didn't have AIDS, and she certainly didn't say she did. But then he went inside and saw Arien alone at her table, picking at her food.

Payton turned red in the face, yelled, grabbed the edge of a lunch table where six juniors were sitting, and flipped it over, spilling their lunches onto the floor. The other football players milled around him, backing him up, and Payton stalked out of the cafeteria. The group of guys followed him out into the hall, where he ranted and raved about that low-down, lyin', sneakin' Arien Belle. They could hear him in the cafeteria, and after about five minutes, Arien got up, dumped her tray, went to her car in the parking lot, and left school.

I couldn't believe that story. Why did Arien tell

Melanie, of all people? No one would have believed Melanie's suspicions. After all, Arien looked as normal and healthy as anyone in school. She even looked *better* than most girls. So why did she tell?

Everyone at school was dying with curiosity, and I shouldn't have been surprised when Andrea called me at home. "So?" she blurted out. "What's this I hear about your pal Arien? Does she really have AIDS?"

"She has the HIV virus," I muttered. "Don't jump off the deep end, Andrea."

"She told the whole senior cafeteria," Andrea went on. "I hear she nearly caused a riot."

"Everybody overreacted," I explained. "Didn't you listen at all in assembly the other day? She can't give it to anybody."

"It's the same thing as AIDS," Andrea said. "So it's just a matter of time."

How could she be so cold about everything? Was Andrea really so jealous of my friendship with Arien that she could be so cruel?

"How can you say that?" I asked. "AIDS is a fatal disease, you know. Arien will die from it."

"Well, she's not going to die tomorrow," Andrea said, offended. "I know it's serious, but those people can live for years."

"Well, *those people* are sick," I answered. "And how

would you feel if you knew you only had one or two years left? And that you'd be terribly, terribly sick for the time you had left?"

Andrea was quiet, so I went on: "What if you knew you'd never get married? Have kids? Or even get your driver's license?"

"All right, I'm sorry."

I snorted into the phone. "You should be. Honestly, Andrea, I think you've been spending too much time with Eric Brandt. You've lost your sense of decency."

That did it. "If I want your opinion, I'll ask for it," Andrea snapped. She hung up.

I went down to the kitchen hoping Uncle Jacob would be there. His gruffness always made me feel better, but he was out for the day, Mom told me. He had to do some work on his column at the newspaper office.

Mom was heating up one of Uncle Jacob's casseroles, and Tom came in the door carrying a grocery bag. "Chicken livers and peanut butter, just like you ordered," he said, kissing Mom on the cheek. "With a jar of butterscotch sauce."

"That's gross, Mom," I said, watching Tom put the things away. "Don't pregnant women ever crave pizza or sub sandwiches or something I like?"

"No," Tom answered. He came up behind Mom,

put his arms around her, and tenderly patted her bulging belly. "And how is little girl Harris today?" he said, nuzzling her ear.

I felt sick.

After dinner, I went upstairs and lay on my bed, face down. My brain was too tired to think, but questions kept spinning around and around in my mind. More than anything this year, I had wanted to be Arien Belle's friend. But how could I be her friend now? It seemed like somehow I had come to a dead end.

I heard Mom's voice calling from downstairs. "Cassie, honey, you've got company." Who could that be? I sat up and shook my hair out of my eyes. "It's Chip, Cassie."

I grabbed my hairbrush, swung it through my hair a couple of times, checked my face, and grabbed a stick of gum from my purse, just in case my breath still smelled like Uncle Jacob's casserole. I ran down the stairs, two steps at a time.

"Hi," Chip said, smiling at me. "I was just congratulating your mother."

"What for?" I asked, then I remembered. "Oh, that. Come on in the library. We can talk in there."

Mom left us alone and we went into the library and sat on the couch. Chip looked around at all the books. "Does anyone actually read these things?" he asked.

"No," I giggled. "But they're here just in case Tom ever needs them."

Chip reached out and held my hand. "I thought maybe you'd want to talk about what happened in school today," he said. "At least now I understand what's been on your mind lately. You knew, didn't you?"

I nodded and my eyes filled with tears, so I looked down at the carpet so Chip wouldn't see. "Yeah, I knew," I said. "But I didn't know what to do about it."

"You don't have to do anything," Chip said, squeezing my hand. "Except keep on being Arien's friend like you have been."

I looked up in surprise. "I can't do that," I gasped. "First of all, she's got AIDS."

"You can't catch AIDS from someone," Chip said. "You know that."

"It's a pretty new disease," I countered. "The doctors don't know everything, do they?"

"They know enough to know you can't get it through casual contact," Chip said smoothly.

"OK, even if I can't get it from her, I just don't know what to say to her. Things are so different now, I don't know how to treat her."

"What's changed?" Chip asked. "You still like a lot of the same things. The things you liked in her haven't changed."

"But she's *dying!*"

"So?" Chip's voice grew softer. "We will all die sometime, and every day we live is one less day we have. We're all dying, but we don't think about it. In Arien's case, we've all just thought about it a little more."

I bit my lower lip. "Maybe I just liked her because she was important at school. Now she's not important anymore. Everyone will hate her."

Chip shook his head. "That's not true, Cassie. You didn't like Arien because of her reputation at school. In fact, you hardly spent any time at all with her at school. And people don't hate her; they're just afraid."

"Why did she tell, Chip?" I looked into his eyes, hoping to find an answer. "She didn't have to tell, and no one would have believed Melanie. So why did she tell?"

Chip shook his head. "I don't know. Maybe she just didn't want to pretend. Maybe she wanted to let them know AIDS was something that could happen to anyone. Maybe she was just really brave and didn't want to pretend it wasn't happening to her."

Chip let go of my hand and slipped his arm around me. He hugged me to his side and whispered in my ear: "Why don't you go ask her?"

I shook my head. "I just can't," I whispered back. "Not now."

14

School was a circus the next day. When Tom dropped me off, there was a large group of parents and kids out on the front sidewalk holding signs that read, Keep the AIDS Virus Away from Our Kids. Another one said, Just Say No to Students with AIDS.

"What's this about?" Tom said, peering out the window.

"Nothing much," I answered, getting out. "There's a rumor that someone in our school has AIDS."

Tom gave a low whistle and shook his head. "If there's going to be legal trouble, I hope they don't call on my law firm to represent them," he said. "I don't even want to think about AIDS." He waved good-bye and pulled out of the parking lot.

Nearly half of my first period class was absent. "Chickens," Andrea said, looking around at the empty desks. "They were afraid to come to school today."

"I know someone else who's afraid to come to school today," Eric said, grinning at Andrea. "That

135

California slut. The whole football team is mad enough to strangle her. They say Payton probably has AIDS, and all the guys are worried because they all use the same showers."

"That's stupid," I spoke up. I usually ignored Eric Brandt all together, but this was too much. "Payton doesn't have AIDS, and you can't get it from using someone else's shower."

"How do you know so much?" Andrea asked, raising an eyebrow. "Payton's told everyone he and Arien were *very* serious, if you know what I mean."

"I know he doesn't have AIDS," I snapped. "And he can go get a blood test and prove it. I wish he would."

Imagine! Sweet, wonderful Payton, who Arien wanted to marry someday, had turned out to be a lying, vicious jerk. He had told the guys who-knows-what about Arien and was going around pretending to be mad at her. Maybe he was a little scared, like we all were, but that was no reason to ruin Arien's reputation.

"Arien Belle is not a slut." It was an unfamiliar voice, and we all stared at Tommy McLaughlin as he finished speaking. It was the first time he'd ever spoken out in class, and I never dreamed he'd ever have the nerve to answer Eric Brandt.

But he was staring at Eric now, his blue eyes intent

on Eric's face. "Arien Belle is a wonderful girl, and if I ever hear you call her anything again, Brandt, I'll personally——"

"What?" Eric snarled. "What will you do, wimp?"

"I don't know," Tommy said, his face smooth. "But I'll think of something."

"You are such a dweeb," Eric said, curling his fingers into fists. "You don't even know the girl. What have you been doing, worshiping her from afar?"

"I know her very well," Tommy said, not even blinking an eye. I felt a surge of pride run through me. This was more impressive that seeing Tommy do a camel spin! "I've skated with her every day for months, and I'll skate with her today and in the future, too. I'm not afraid."

Eric Brandt's face was stony, but I knew he couldn't answer Tommy. Eric could act tough and rough, but when it came down to it, he was as scared as Payton Wardell. Tommy McLaughlin, our class misfit, had more courage than all of us put together.

Tommy turned in my direction, and I looked down at my notebook while my cheeks burned. I was Arien's friend, too, and I hadn't even gone to see her. I was just like the rest of them, absolutely terrified of an invisible virus and of the girl who carried it.

The story made the newspaper that evening. I was studying upstairs in my room when Mom came in, carrying the paper. "Cassie," she said, carefully lowering herself into the wing chair in my room, "the paper says someone at your school has AIDS. There were a lot of protesters at school today and a lot of kids were absent. Is that right?"

I nodded. "That's right, but it's silly. The person wasn't even in school today. I don't know if they'll ever come back."

"Do you know who this person is? The paper doesn't say."

"It shouldn't have to say, Mom. That's a violation of privacy, isn't it?"

Mom knew I was evading the question. "Cassie, surely you've heard a rumor. Who is it?"

I put down my pencil. I might as well tell her. The ladies at the country club would tell her tonight or tomorrow or next week even if I didn't. "It's Arien Belle."

"Arien? *Your* Arien?"

"Yes."

Mom went as white as my notebook paper. She leaned back in the chair, put her hands on her belly, and gasped. "You're kidding. You've been hanging around this girl every day for weeks——you were even with her when she got sick!"

"I know, Mom. But I can't get it from her."

"When she was sick—did she throw up? Did any of it get on you? Did you share drinks with her? Did she ever have a nosebleed or a cut—and did you get her blood on you?"

I crinkled my nose. "Gross, Mom. That's disgusting."

"Cassie." Mom was firm now. "I've got to know. I'm thinking about this baby. Babies can get AIDS, you know, if their mothers have the virus. And if you got it and gave it to me, then this baby—" Her chin quivered and she broke out in loud sobs. "Oh, my goodness," she cried, "I've shaken her hand. At the skating rink. I shook her hand."

Tom came running up the stairs. "What's wrong?" he yelled, rushing into my room. "Claire? Are you OK?"

"The girl with AIDS is Cassie's friend, and I shook her hand," Mom sobbed. "Tom, what if the baby's been exposed?"

Tom took Mom's hands and pulled her out of the chair. As he led her out of the room, he made quiet, soothing noises. When she was out in the hall, he turned and looked at me like I had suddenly turned green or something. He reached for the door and pulled it shut behind him.

It was my weekend to go to Dad's condo, and I

think Mom was relieved to see me go. I couldn't help but notice that she had begun doing little things that made me feel contaminated—she had told Uncle Jacob to wash my dishes separately, she stayed twenty feet away from me, and she didn't kiss me good-bye when Dad came to pick me up. She probably even put on plastic gloves when she washed my laundry. "It's ridiculous," I told Dad and Max. Both of them were scientific types, and I knew they wouldn't be as crazy about the AIDS scare as everyone else. "I feel like I'm diseased or something."

"You have to understand what your mother's going through," Dad said, steering his new red convertible sports car into the condo parking lot. "She's thirty-seven and pregnant. Older women have more complications in pregnancy, and she was probably a little scared even before this AIDS thing came up."

"That's right," Max added. "Tom said she even had amniocentesis to see if the baby was genetically OK."

"So?" I asked.

"It is," Max said. "And it's a girl."

A girl. I was going to have a baby sister. Ugh. That meant I'd have to share my room eventually, when she outgrew the nursery. Maybe I could go to college early or something. Or maybe I could move in with Dad and Max. Something would have to happen.

It was actually nice to get away from home and spend time with Dad and Max. I told them everything about Arien, and it felt good to be totally honest with somebody.

"If you really care about your friend," Dad said, his dark eyes gleaming, "you'll be there when she needs you."

Max nodded. "You told me once, Cass, that God never leaves us when the going gets rough," he said. "So why should God's children leave each other when things get rough? Aren't we supposed to help each other?"

Dad and Max were both so logical and well-informed about AIDS that by the time I left to go back home Sunday afternoon, I knew what I wanted to do. Monday, after school, I'd go see Arien at the rink. Every afternoon, as long as she needed a cheering section, I'd be there. Tommy hadn't let her down, and I wouldn't either.

Dad took me home and walked me to the door. We were both surprised to see Mom and Tom standing in the foyer. "Cassie, I'm glad you're home," Mom said simply. "I want you to promise me you will never see Arien Belle again."

"Claire, you can't mean that," Dad interrupted. "Arien needs a friend right now, and I'm very proud that our daughter is courageous enough to want to be that friend."

"Stay out of this, Glen," Mom warned. "I'm thinking of my baby."

"So am I," Dad shot back. "There's no danger to your baby. Trust me. But forbidding Cassie to see Arien would seriously hurt both of them."

Mom turned without speaking and ran up the stairs. Tom watched her go, then turned to Dad. "Are you sure?" he asked. "Claire's a mass of raging hormones just now, but we want to be sure it's safe for Cassie and the baby."

"It's safe," Dad said. He bent down and kissed me on the cheek. "See you later, Gypsy Girl. Keep your promise."

15

On Monday morning, Mom didn't come into my
room and wake me up like she usually did. She
just pounded on the door and yelled, "Cassie! Get
up!"

I groaned. She'd probably be like this for a while.
Dad may have convinced Tom to let me see Arien,
but Mom wasn't going to be convinced so easily.

I gathered my things for school and as I reached
into the closet for my shoes, I saw the brightly
wrapped package I'd bought months ago for Arien's
"birthday party." What a mess that had been! But
somehow it had all worked out because I really got
to know Arien that day.

I put the package into my book bag and zipped
the bag shut, hoping I wasn't too late to reclaim that
friendship.

After school, I walked into the rink. It was quiet,
and Coach Davison seemed surprised to see me.
"Hey, Cassie," he said, smiling. "Long time no see."

"I know," I said, putting my books down on a

table in the snack bar. "It took me a while to come around."

The coach nodded grimly. "I know. Lots of people haven't come around yet. The parents of every single kid in the Tuesday-Thursday skating classes have canceled their kids' lessons because Arien's a helper."

"Wow." It seemed terrible, but I knew from experience how people reacted to AIDS. "Couldn't you just ask Arien not to help?"

Coach Davison winked at me. "I won't do that. She's a fine part of this skating program, and I'm not going to cut her out now."

Arien came out of the ladies' room and skated out onto the rink without glancing up. "Hey, Arien," Coach yelled. "Your cheering section has arrived."

She looked up in surprise and saw me. "Really?" With a few powerful strokes, she skated over to the rail at the edge of the rink. "Do you want to talk to me from here, or can I come sit down?" she asked.

I blushed. "Come sit down here," I said, slipping into the booth. "I've got a lot to tell you."

Tommy McLaughlin came in, and Coach yelled at him to practice his figures. "Arien's been here for an hour already," Coach bellowed. "She'll join you after her break."

Arien slid into the booth across from me. "I

brought you something," I said, pulling the present from my book bag. "Happy birthday."

Arien was puzzled. "My birthday's in October."

"I know." I laughed. "Remember that day I showed up here and said I confused the time of a birthday party? Melanie Sergeant told me the party was for you. It was all a big joke. She didn't have any idea you'd actually be here."

"So you bought this present for me—way back then?"

"Yeah. I was going to save it until October, but I thought I'd give it to you now." I bit my lip—that was probably the wrong thing to say.

"Because I might not be around in October?" Arien said, brightly. "It's OK, Cassie, believe me. I love un-birthday presents."

She unwrapped the paper and lifted the box lid. The sweater was just as soft as I'd remembered, but I'd forgotten there was so much golden sparkle in the weave. "It's gorgeous," Arien sighed. "Thanks so much! With an aqua skating skirt, I could wear this at the regional."

"You're welcome." She put the sweater carefully back into the box, and I asked the question I had to ask: "Arien, why did you tell everyone?"

She carefully put the lid back on the box, then crumpled the wrapping paper and held it in her hand, a tight wad. "I thought about the future," she said. "About how in a year or two or three I'd be gone, and everyone would gather and look at the yearbook. They would all know then, probably, and they'd be able to figure it out. I just didn't want to be known forever as the girl who lied to her classmates."

"But they wouldn't know," I said slowly, thinking it through. "Not if you went back to California. They'd just think they lost touch with you."

Arien shook her head. "No, they'd know. Payton was going to go to college with me, you see, and we were going to get married." Her voice broke, and I realized for the first time how deeply Payton had hurt her. "So I knew they'd know. Eventually."

"I'm so sorry," I whispered.

"For what?"

"That this happened. About Payton. And that I didn't come to see you. I was afraid."

"It's OK," she said, smiling up at me. "I was afraid too, that whole first week. I kept thinking that I must really be a cruddy person for God to let this happen to me. I thought about when I was younger, when I was doing drugs. We shared needles then, all the time, and I'm sure that's how I got this. Last week my dad looked for the guy I did drugs with and found out he died two years ago."

"It doesn't seem fair," I said, looking at her perfect face. She looked like a Miss America, not a druggie. "You've changed so much since those days."

"Yes, I have," Arien said, "and the best change of all was when I gave my life to God a few weeks ago. Thanks to you, Cass. Since then I've been reading my Bible, and I really have a peace about whatever comes. All I want to do is my best in what I'm doing. Right now, that's skating. I'm going to bring a gold medal back to Coach Davison if it's the last thing I do." She shrugged and twirled a wheel of her skate absently. "He's stuck with me through everything, and he deserves it."

"What about school?" I asked.

Arien sighed. "I'm going to finish school with a private tutor. I can't go back there."

"I don't blame you," I said. "It's not worth it."

"Not for only two more months," she said. "But the regional is right around the corner, and Tommy and I have a lot of work to do. I am *not* going to be sick during that competition!"

I felt better when I saw her determination. If anyone could pull it off, Arien could. She stood up, ready to go practice with Tommy, and I pulled out my books to do my homework. But before she left, she leaned over to whisper in my ear, and it took every bit of my self-control not to pull away.

"Do you know something?" she said. "I told Tommy about accepting Christ as my Savior, thinking, you know, that he'd want to do it too. But he said he had done it when he was six years old!" She laughed and shook her head in bewilderment. "Can you imagine? We're together all the time, and he never mentioned *anything* to me."

She skated away then, and I looked up at the ceiling. "Thanks, God," I whispered. "I'm glad I talked to her when I did, even if Max was the one who brought it up."

I tackled my homework, looking up every now and then to see Tommy and Arien skating with an energy I'd never noticed before. It was as though they knew the coming competition would be their last—and every second counted.

16

When it became clear that Arien Belle was not going to return to school, things calmed down. The parent protesters left, Melanie Sergeant was cool and smug again as leader of the senior girls, and our figure improvement class seemed dull and boring without Arien's enthusiastic example.

She had left her mark, though. Even though most people didn't want to talk about her, I think all of us were more aware that we weren't immortal. We weren't going to live forever.

In English class, Miss Chamberlain pulled out her poetry book. "Thanatology is the study of death," she began. "The root *thana* refers to death. What, then, would the poem 'Thanatopsis' be about?"

It was a simple question, but no one raised a hand. I rolled my eyes and finally did, or I knew we'd be sitting there for five minutes in silence. "Death," I said when she nodded at me.

"You're right, Cassie," she said. "William Cullen

Bryant wrote 'Thanatopsis' in 1821. It's a long poem, but I'd like to read the last stanza for you."

Eric Brandt put his head down on his desk and pretended to sleep. Andrea covered her mouth, stifling a giggle, and I propped my head on my hand, sighing. I couldn't help but notice, though, that Tommy McLaughlin was actually listening for a change.

Miss Chamberlain read:

> *"So live, that when thy summons comes to join*
> *The innumerable caravan which moves*
> *To that mysterious realm, where each shall take*
> *His chamber in the silent halls of death,*
> *Thou go not, like the quarry slave at night,*
> *Scourged to his dungeon, but, sustained and soothed*
> *By an unfaltering trust, approach thy grave,*
> *Like one who wraps the drapery of his couch*
> *About him, and lies down to pleasant dreams."*

Miss Chamberlain put her book in her lap and looked at us. I groaned. She was going to ask another question, and no one but me would answer. Deja vu.

"The poet is using a metaphor, comparing death to something," she said. "What is the metaphor?"

Tommy McLaughlin raised his hand before I even

had a chance to. Miss Chamberlain raised an eyebrow and nodded at Tommy.

"He's saying death is just like taking a nap," Tommy said. "That if you approach death with trust instead of fear, you don't have to worry about it."

Miss Chamberlain nodded and smiled slightly. "Very good, Tommy. But there's another metaphor in the poem, too. What did Mr. Bryant mean when he wrote that death is 'an innumerable caravan which moves to that mysterious realm'?"

I raised my hand. "It's like death comes for all of us at one time or another," I answered. "It doesn't wipe us out or anything, we just join up with the caravan and move from one place to another."

"Excellent. For your homework tonight—" she paused for our collective groan— "I want you to memorize that last stanza. You'll find it on page 114 of your textbook. Tomorrow morning you will write it for me from memory."

She glanced up at the clock. "That's all for today, so why don't you get started on the poem? When the bell rings, you are dismissed."

Miss Chamberlain left the room on one of those mysterious errands teachers sometimes run when they're supposed to be in class. Andrea giggled and winked at Eric. "She's probably gone for a quick smoke in the teacher's lounge," she said.

Eric and his buddies laughed at Andrea, and I looked back at Chip. He was reading a new book, *The Mind of Your Dog*.

"How's it going at the vet's?" I asked.

"Fine," he said, looking up. "This stuff is really interesting."

I could tell he didn't want to be bothered. I looked around lazily. Tommy had stacked his books, ready for the bell, and I couldn't help but notice on the top of his English book lay a Bible. A shiny, red Holy Bible.

Wow. Tommy was carrying a Bible to school! Did this have something to do with Arien? Did he feel guilty for not ever telling Arien he was a Christian?

I wasn't the only one who noticed the Bible. Eric Brandt, his buddies, and Andrea all noticed it, too.

"Hey!" Eric yelled. "Bozo's got a Bible! A nice shiny red one! Hey, Bozo, are you on your way to Sunday school?"

The comments began to fly through the air.

"What's the idea, Bozo?"

"He's been reading the Ten Commandments, man. 'Thou shalt be a dweeb.'"

"Thou shalt be nice to the teachers."

"Thou shalt be a goody-two-shoes."

"Thou shalt be a narc as often as possible."

Eric fell to his knees in the aisle, the center of

attention. He clasped his hands, as if he was praying. "Help me, Lord," he whimpered theatrically, gazing at the ceiling and pretending to cry. "Help the big bullies not to pick on me because I'm a bozo."

Every eye turned toward Tommy, who until then had simply sat with his back to Eric. But now he stood up, his face pale and his eyes steely blue. He faced Eric and with one hand picked up the Bible.

"If you're so tough and cool," Tommy said, looking down at Eric, who was still on his knees, "*you* carry it."

Tommy held the Bible out to Eric, who froze. Tommy's hand trembled with some emotion; I didn't know if it was anger, fear, or just excitement.

Eric stiffened, his eyes darting around the room, then he smiled and relaxed. "Hey," he said, standing up. "It was just a joke. Don't take it personally, man."

Tommy took a step closer to Eric, still holding out the Bible, and Eric threw his hands up defensively. "Hey, I don't want your Bible, man. I can see it means a lot to you. It's cool, and I'm sorry."

Tommy's hand with the Bible dropped to his side, and he nodded at Eric. But the glint of determination never left his eye. The bell rang, and we all gathered our books and left, but I realized it was one of the few times I had ever seen the real person inside

Tommy McLaughlin. I wished Arien could have seen it, too.

I told her all about it that afternoon at the rink. She glowed and yelled, "All right, Tommy!" when I told her how Tommy stopped Eric by literally offering him the Bible.

"Did you have anything to do with that?" I asked her. "Did you encourage him to take his Bible to school?"

Arien shook her head. "I don't think so. I did give him a hard time about not telling me about Jesus, though. And I've been talking a lot about the things I'm learning from the Bible. My mom got me some good Bible-study books at a bookstore, and I'm reading some fascinating things, Cassie. But I didn't tell Tommy to take his Bible to school."

"Well, whatever happened to Tommy, it's pretty fantastic," I said. "He's not the same kid. He didn't even sleep in class today."

"I only wish I could talk him into trying out for a solo in the competition," Arien sighed. "He's doing figures and the dances with me, but he just won't do anything by himself. He's *great* on skates, probably even better than me, but he just doesn't have any confidence in himself."

I shrugged. "Maybe it'll come later. He's still young, you know." I giggled. Here we were, like two old women, discussing Tommy like he was a little kid, when he and I were the same age.

Arien smiled, too. "Yeah. He's got lots of years ahead of him. He'll be a national champion yet, you wait and see."

Coach Davison blew his whistle, and it was time for Arien to get out on the rink. Tommy came off and skated behind the snack bar counter for a drink.

"You're looking great," I called to him as Arien left. "You ought to go out for solo dance or freestyle, you know."

Tommy was startled that I was talking to him, but he smiled and shook his head. "Naw," he said. "I like dance. Everyone just looks at the girl."

He had a point. I shrugged and went back to working on memorizing "Thanatopsis." It was easier if I wrote it down, and all day I'd been writing it on slips of paper, trying to get the words right.

Arien came toward the edge of the rink and I heard her skates *thump* against the siderails. "Hey, Cassie," she called. "Tommy and I need some help."

"What?"

"We took the voices out of 'That's What Friends Are For,'" she said, "for one of our dances. But we could use some inspiration. Go to the mike, will you, and sing it for us?"

I was about to automatically say no, because I

155

don't ever want people to think I like to show off. But then I thought, *Why not?* Arien wouldn't think I was a show-off. She was my friend.

I walked over to the sound booth and waited for the music to begin. Arien and Tommy went to their starting positions, flexed their bodies, and Coach started the song.

I sang and watched as words, music, and movement all came together. It was an incredible combination. Just last month I'd seen this same routine, and it looked like a series of movements. Now, though, Tommy and Arien flowed together across the rink like rippling water, effortlessly. They were perfect together.

They closed the routine with a few graceful movements that matched the simple harmonica music at the end of the song. Together they went into beautiful camel spins, then slowed, and came down in a bow.

I burst into applause, and Arien looked up, grinning. "Quit it," she teased. "You'll make us overconfident."

Tommy actually spoke. "That was nice, Cassie," he said, looking down at the floor. "It really helps."

"Get back to your starting positions," Coach Davison called, "and I'll cue up the song again. We've got to do it about twenty more times today."

I groaned. "You don't have to sing it every time, Cassie," Coach said. "I wouldn't want your voice to get tired."

I grabbed a stool and perched on it near the microphone. "It's OK," I said, as the music played again. "On the day of victory, no one is tired, right?"

Coach gave me a puzzled look, but I just started singing, thinking of how Tommy stood up to Eric Brandt. It was Tommy's day of victory, for sure.

17

School ended with a whimper instead of a bang, at least for me. There just wasn't anything exciting about it. Next year would just be more of the same thing as this year, except with different teachers. Everything really important in my life had nothing to do with school. Mom's baby was due in September, which meant things at home would become more and more baby-ized, the regional skating competition was in early June, and the national was in late July.

Mom was six months pregnant and considered it some kind of a milestone. She still stayed a healthy distance away from me, and I pretended not to notice that she made Uncle Jacob wash my dishes twice in the dishwasher before they were used again. She never went in my room or came near me. I understood, but I have to admit it hurt my feelings a little.

I wondered myself. What if the doctors are wrong and somehow I did get AIDS? I was never really close to Arien—we didn't share drinks anymore, and usu-ally she was sixty feet away in the rink while I stayed either in the snack bar or in the sound booth. We didn't touch, we didn't hug, we didn't share hairbrushes. I never touched her sweaty socks or put on her skates. I was pretty sure I was safe.

But every now and then I'd run my hand over my throat to see if I could be getting sick. Did I have a fever? When I caught a summer cold the week after school was out, I was really scared for a couple of days—and so was Mom. She became extra-hyper, and I started leaving for the skating rink at noon so I'd be out of her hair all day. I was sick of hearing about baby stuff, anyway.

I went to the rink three days before the regional with a cold. I was carrying a box of tissues, a bottle of cough syrup, and a tea bag. (The tea bag was Uncle Jacob's suggestion.) Arien and Tommy were already on the rink, practicing a dance, and Arien saw me and called out, "Hey, Cass! Going to sing for me today?"

"Can't," I called back, sounding like a stuffed-up Daffy Duck. "I got a code in my nodse."

They whirled away from me and I settled myself on the stool in the sound booth. Coach Davison looked at me curiously. "Got a cold?" he asked, look-ing worried.

How sweet of him to be concerned. "Yes." I nodded, sniffing for emphasis. "But I'll be OK."

"Stay away from Arien, will you?" He turned back
to watch Tommy and Arien, and I was shocked for a
minute. Stay away from Arien? Could I catch AIDS
from her when my resistance was down?

I grabbed my box of tissues. "I just remembered,"
I said, practically falling off my stool. "I've got somewhere to go. See you tomorrow."

Coach Davison nodded, and I made tracks to the
phone to call for a ride home.

The regional competition for the southeastern
United States was to be held in Orlando on Saturday.
On Friday, safely over my cold, I went to the rink
early to see Arien. I wanted more than anything to
see her win a gold medal in Orlando.

"Hi," I called, seeing her on the figure eight
painted on the rink floor. "Are you ready for tomorrow?"

"As ready as I'll ever be," she answered evenly,
while gliding smoothly around the tiny painted
circle. She was amazing. Every muscle in her body
was in perfect alignment. She had absolutely perfect
control.

I looked around. We were alone. "Where's Tommy
and Coach?" I asked.

"Gone to the sporting goods store," she answered, leading off on another circle.

"Oh." I smiled happily, glad to be here instead of at home. "I couldn't stay home another minute," I babbled. "Max is there today, watching the baby kick the inside of Mom's belly. Can you believe it? He was playing different kinds of music to see the baby's reaction, and Mom was actually putting up with it. She thought it was cute!" I shook my head. "I'm absolutely sick of all this baby stuff. I hate that Mom's pregnant."

Arien abruptly jerked her free foot and turned in one quick movement toward me. In an instant, she had skated over, and she stood five inches from me, glaring at me in pure anger.

"Cassie Perkins, I'm sick and tired of hearing you gripe about that baby!" she whispered, her hand shaking on the rail. "It's a new life, can't you see it? Life is precious, or don't you realize it? How can you stand there and say you hate an innocent baby? How dare you!"

She turned then, and skated in a wide, fast circle around the rink, her arms beating the air furiously. I was shocked, then I realized what my griping must have seemed like to her. "Wait," I yelled, ducking under the rail and running into the rink. "Stop, Arien!"

I ran after her, but she was just too fast. I ran and ran in circles, like an idiot, while she burned off her anger whipping around the rink. Finally her legs stopped pumping, and she covered her face with her hands as she circled the rink. Her shoulders were shaking.

I stood in the center of the rink and waited for her to pass by. When she did, I stepped into her path and she crashed into me. *Wham!* We both went down in a pile. "Are you *nuts?*" Arien screamed. "Do you want me to break a leg the day before the regional? Or maybe you'd just like me to be covered with bruises so I'll look really good."

"No," I cried, confused and sorry. "I just wanted to stop you. I'm sorry, Arien, I didn't want to make you mad."

"That's not all that makes me mad," she said, yanking her hand out from under my arm. She pulled herself up to a sitting position. "Sometimes the unfairness of everything builds up inside me like a boil, and then it just explodes."

"That's gross."

"Life's gross." But then she looked at me and saw that I was smiling. She looked up at the ceiling in exasperation. "Well, sometimes life is gross."

I stretched out on my side and propped my head up with my hand. "I've never seen you so angry."

Arien's smile was twisted. "The other night I got so mad I destroyed my room—tore all the sheets off the bed, yanked pictures off the wall, and broke a lamp. Mom came in, looked around, and handed me a picture off the wall I'd missed." She laughed. "I guess everybody reaches a boiling point every now and then."

"You're a fighter, Arien. Maybe that's good. Maybe it will help you not to get sick, you know, so soon. You can fight it off."

Arien shook her head. "That's another reason I was mad at you. When you started griping about the baby, that was just the thing that set me off. But the other day I was so mad, I could have killed you."

This was news to me. I sat up. "What did I do?"

Arien leaned toward me—I gritted my teeth again, trying not to pull away involuntarily—and she knocked on my forehead with her fist. "Hello?" she asked. "Anybody in there? Didn't you realize that when you have a cold, I could get it? And that a cold is lots more dangerous to me than to you? You went home that day, which I appreciated, but not until Coach told you to."

"Coach didn't tell me to go home," I whispered, remembering. "I thought if I had a cold, I could get AIDS more easily. I'm so sorry."

Arien lay back on the floor of the rink, her hand

covering her eyes. I felt like the world's biggest, dumbest fool. I had been so self-centered! Griping about the baby because I was jealous and selfish, thinking about my health instead of Arien's—

"All I ever wanted to be was your friend," I whispered.

"Some friend," Arien mumbled, still covering her eyes. I could see tears shining on her cheek. "You're scared to death of me just like everyone else."

I looked down at the floor, then reached up with my hand and gently wiped the tears from her cheek. The AIDS virus could be in tears, right? But it wasn't transmitted that way, right? OK, there. I wasn't afraid.

Arien stiffened when she felt me touch her. She lay still for a minute, then took her hand away from her eyes. "No one has touched me in weeks," she said, her eyes swimming in tears. "Except Mom, Tommy, and those doctors who won't do it unless they're wearing plastic gloves. Not even Coach Davison."

I wiped her other cheek as well, a little clumsily. "What are friends for?" I asked. "Now you'd better get busy. You've got a medal to win tomorrow."

18

The next day I stood with Coach Davison and watched Tommy and Arien skate their way through the preliminaries toward the finals. Tommy had really changed in the last few weeks. He even looked taller now, and he carried himself with confidence although he still ducked his head shyly if anyone asked him a direct question. He was gentle and protective toward Arien, even though she teased him constantly about being too shy to compete in a solo event.

In the rink for the dance team competition, they looked like a golden couple. In the figures Arien had worn the sweater I got her and a skating skirt, but now she was wearing a new outfit spangled with sequins, embroidery, and Illusion lace.

They danced through the competition as if they had been skating together their entire lives. "They actually look like they're having fun," I remarked to Coach Davison.

He grinned, watching his two stars. "I think they are," he answered.

The competition was stiff. Another couple from Atlanta, Georgia, was just as thrilling as Tommy and Arien, and they were last year's gold medal winners. Their experience showed in their attitude. While Tommy and Arien looked natural and happy, the other couple looked natural and proud. When the dance competition was over, the Atlanta couple had won the gold medal; Tommy and Arien won the silver. But they qualified for the national competition in July.

That morning in figures Tommy won a silver in the men's division, and Arien won a bronze in the women's. As Arien waited for her solo freestyle competition, I knew what she was thinking—she only had one more chance to bring home a gold medal today. If she didn't win one today, she'd have to wait until the national championship in July.

It was an exhausting competition. I was tired to the bone, and I hadn't even done anything. Coach Davison was tired, too, and there were little puffy bags under his eyes. Tommy seemed pleasantly satisfied with his performance now that his work was done. But Arien was supercharged. She had one more event, and she was hyped.

An hour before her freestyle event, Mrs. Belle brought hamburgers for all of us, but Arien was too nervous to eat. "I don't have an appetite," she told her mother.

"Are you feeling OK?" Mrs. Belle asked, worried. She put her hand on Arien's forehead, but Arien brushed it off. "Just nerves, Mom. I'm OK."

When her turn came, I was afraid she was too excited to do well—she had to have her power under control, and she seemed so hyper I thought she'd fly off and do triple jumps instead of the double jumps that were required.

"Calm down!" I whispered in her ear as she stood on the brink of the rink. "Just think of that cool gold medal."

"Gold isn't cool, Cass," Arien answered, taking a deep breath. "It's hot!" She pushed off into the rink, and we watched her give the best performance of her life.

But it wasn't quite good enough for gold. Another skater beat her by a tenth of a point, and Arien stood on the silver medal platform to receive a bouquet of roses and a silver medal.

"That's OK," I heard Tommy tell Coach Davison. "There's still the national. She can do it."

"I hope so," Mrs. Belle answered. "It's what she's living for."

Mrs. Belle insisted that Arien take two weeks off before beginning training for the national competition in Lewisville, Texas. "That will be a strenuous trip," she told Arien on our way home from the regional. "And you and I are going to meet your father in the Bahamas for two weeks. You can walk on the beach and relax and swim and have fun. Anything, but no skating."

Arien rolled her eyes and winked at me. I knew she'd probably find a gym in the hotel or somewhere and work out the entire time. But hey, who wouldn't like to spend two weeks in the Bahamas?

"Well, I won't be home for a while either," I told her. "Mom's arranged for me to spend the summer with Dad and Max at the condo. It's a visitation rights deal," I explained, although privately I thought it had more to do with getting me out of the house than having me spend time with Dad. I didn't mind, though. Dad and Max were good company. We'd eat Italian food every night, and I'd sleep on the beach every day.

"What are you going to do, Tommy?" Arien asked.

Tommy ducked his head. "Skate, I guess," he answered.

Coach Davison laughed. "All of Florida could be evacuated in a hurricane alert, and everyone would leave except Tommy," he said, patting Tommy's shoulder. "He'd be skating."

"I still think you should go out for a solo event,"

Arien told him, leaning forward in the car. "There's a new category, solo dance, and since you've already qualified for the national in two events, you could enter, even now. Come on, Tommy, do it!"

Tommy grinned, but shook his head. "No," he said. "Not this year."

Arien and I looked at each other. Tommy may have changed a lot, but he wasn't about to break completely out of his shell.

19

I heard the phone ringing in the middle of the night and glanced up at my digital clock that glowed through the darkness. Three-thirty. Who would call at three-thirty in the morning?

Dad knocked on my door. "Cass, it's about your mother," he said. "She's gone into labor."

"What?" I sat up, feeling curiously wide-awake. "It's too early. The baby isn't due for another two months."

"I know." Dad's voice was oddly flat. "Tom said the doctors are optimistic, but they're still very concerned about the baby. We can go to the hospital tomorrow."

"OK." Dad closed my door and left, and I slipped out of bed and knelt by the side of my bed. Suddenly the baby wasn't just an annoyance, she was my baby sister and she was in trouble. "Please, God," I prayed. "I'm sorry for everything I ever said or felt about this baby. Please let her be OK. Please let Mom be OK, and Tom, and Nick, and Uncle Jacob, and

Max, and everyone who wanted this baby. Please, God, I'm so sorry."

It was quiet in my room, and I didn't know if God would answer my prayer or not. Maybe the baby wasn't ready to be born and she would be better off in heaven. Maybe she was a fighter, like Arien, and she'd pull through. But maybe she wasn't.

I'd had a postcard from Arien. "Staying another two weeks here on the beach," she had written. "See you in July." Well, maybe I wouldn't be seeing her just yet. My baby sister needed me.

Dad walked me and Max up to the hospital ward where they kept the premature babies. Tom was there in the outer waiting room, looking rumpled and scruffy. He looked like he hadn't shaved in three days. "Hi, Tom," I said gently. "How's the baby?"

Tom jerked his head toward a glass wall that separated the waiting room from the sterile environment of the preemie nursery. "They don't know," he said, looking down at the floor.

"What's her name?" Max asked.

"We haven't named her yet," Tom said, nearly choking on the words. "Your mother and I wanted to wait until she was born to see what she looked like." He looked back down at the floor. "I guess we'll wait until she's stronger."

I nodded, then walked over to the nursery

window. "Cass," I heard my dad say, "I'm going on to work, OK? I'll just leave you and Max with Tom. Call me when you're ready to come home."

I waved good-bye to Dad, then peered in the nursery window again. Max was watching the medical machines in fascination, and I looked at the little bundled babies in the clear incubators. They looked like little baby dolls in gigantic clear plastic shoeboxes, with wires and tubes running all around them.

A nurse in a sterile green hospital gown, cap, and mask, looked over at me and smiled with her eyes. She pointed toward the incubators and raised her eyebrows. I nodded. "Harris," I mouthed.

She nodded as if she understood and wheeled one of the incubators closer to the window. "Baby girl Harris," a large card said at the foot of the tiny bed. Inside, a tiny bundled baby in a pink stocking cap daintily stretched her fingers in the air. She opened her eyes and I gasped. "What blue eyes," I whispered to Max.

"Dummy," he said, his eyes never leaving our new sister. "All newborns have blue eyes."

Tom stood behind us, watching too. "She weighed in at five pounds, three ounces," he said, a little proudly. "The doctors think she'll be fine, and they said she can go home when she gains just five more ounces."

Two little circles were stuck on her tiny chest, and a machine near her bed beeped steadily, recording her heartbeats. "She's a strong little thing," I said, watching the tiny green dot on the screen that bounced with each beep.

"They're just concerned about her lungs," Tom said. "If she can breathe on her own, they think she'll be fine."

I think I could have stayed there all day. Imagine! That tiny little person had been inside my mother just yesterday, but here she was now, part of the human race.

"One day old," I whispered to Max. "Imagine it."

"Actually, no, Cassie," Max explained, in the voice he used for explanations. "She's only twenty-eight weeks old. You can't compare a preemie to a baby that was born on schedule. Babies who arrive on schedule are really nine months old when they're born, but she's only seven months."

I rolled my eyes in exasperation, and Tom laughed. He put his hands on our shoulders, and for the first time I actually felt sort of close to him. "You two have made me feel a lot better," he said, rubbing Max's head. "She's going to have a great time with her older brothers and sister."

Brothers? I had almost forgotten that Nick would be her brother, too. Nick came into the waiting room then, carrying an arrangement of flowers. "I got the ones you wanted, Dad," he said, holding up the bouquet. "Can we see Claire now?"

"Don't you want to see the baby?" I asked.

Nick put the flowers down on a chair and stood in front of the window, as gaga as the rest of us. He watched her blink, open her fingers, and finally, yawn.

We all laughed. "I think she's bored with us," Tom said. "Let's go see your mother."

Mom was sitting up in bed, surrounded by flowers already. Uncle Jacob was sitting in a chair, an arrangement of daisies on his lap. "Really, Tom, more flowers?" she said with a laugh when she saw Nick carrying another bouquet. "I'm going to start sneezing if this keeps up."

She smiled at us, but her eyes met Tom's and I could see that she was intensely serious. "How is she?" she asked, trying not to sound worried.

Tom sat on the edge of the bed and took Mom's hands. "She's doing great. The doctors say she's fine; they just want to make sure she gains a little more weight before they let us take her home. Just five more ounces, Claire, then she's all ours."

Mom closed her eyes and shook her head. "I just want to hold her."

"I'm sure it won't be long," Tom soothed her.

We kids stood around awkwardly, not knowing what to say. "She's beautiful, Mom," I said finally. "I think she could probably even wear my old Cabbage Patch doll's clothes. She's so delicate!"

"She's got blue eyes," Nick said.

"All babies have blue eyes at first," Max repeated again, a little impatiently. "Sometimes they change color."

"Five pounds, three ounces," Mom murmured, looking at Tom. "She would have been a big baby if I'd carried her until September."

"A giant," Max inserted. "But the lightest surviving infant weighed just ten ounces when it was born. So our baby is simply huge, Mom."

"That can't be true," scoffed Nick. "Ten ounces?"

"It's true," Max insisted. "They fed it with a fountain-pen filler. The biggest baby ever recorded weighed twenty-nine pounds at birth."

Mom groaned. "I'll stick with my five-pounder," she said, smiling at Max. "Now, Max, can't you go find someone else to cheer up?"

"Let's leave your mom and dad alone," Uncle Jacob said, standing up and shooing us toward the door. "I'll take these big kids home, Tom, and dinner will be ready for you at six if you want to come home." He paused. "Call us if anything comes up, OK?"

Tom nodded and held Mom's hands in his. I was feeling so weird, kind of happy and fascinated, that I didn't even correct Uncle Jacob when he called Tom my dad. I guess we really were a family now. We weren't just married together—now we had ties to each other that were deeper. We shared a baby. A tiny, pink, blue-eyed baby with no name—yet.

We were going out the wide double doors of the hospital lobby when I saw a face I recognized. "Mr. Belle," I called, leaving Uncle Jacob and the boys. "You're supposed to be in the Bahamas!"

Mr. Belle nodded, glad to see me. "Hi, Cassie. We came home yesterday."

"Did you have a nice time?" I looked around. "What are you doing here?"

Mr. Belle cleared his throat uneasily and looked away for a minute. "Arien caught a bad cold on our trip," he said. "We brought her home. Last night she broke out in chills and fever. We brought her here, and the doctors have told us she has double pneumonia."

I cleared my throat uneasily. I could tell the situation was serious; Mr. Belle was pale under his tan, and he looked like he hadn't slept in a week. "Can I see her?"

"Not today," Mr. Belle shook his head. "Her mother's with her, and they aren't allowing any other visitors. I'm not even allowed in the room. But check back tomorrow." He started to walk away, but stopped and held up his hand. "Are things OK in your family? Is everyone well?"

I nodded. "My mother had her baby. It was premature, but seems to be doing OK."

"Good." Mr. Belle waved good-bye, and stepped into the elevator.

20

That night I dreamed Max and I flew to Mars. Somehow (you know how weird dreams are) I ejected from our spaceship and was falling through the martian atmosphere. Andy Griffith and Barney Fife were in the air, too, calling out, "Just kick, like you're treading water. Keep those legs pointed and straight, and kick! Kick!"

So I kicked and waved my arms while Max flew around in the spaceship shining a light in my eyes. I heard him say, "It's like amniotic fluid, Cass. Just kick."

But the effort was exhausting, and I had to stop kicking. "I'm tired," I said, and immediately I felt myself begin to fall.

I could see the red martian surface coming up to meet me, and I knew I'd fall flat within seconds. But suddenly, Barney Fife was there, and his skinny arm caught me just as I was about to hit the ground. He didn't pick me back up, though, he just lowered me gently onto the surface.

"Thanks," I told him.

"It was nothing," he said. "That's what friends are for."

I spent most of the next week at the hospital, reading books and working crossword puzzles. I could never finish the crosswords, though, so Max spent all his time filling in my leftover blank spaces.

Just for a while, Max and I had moved back to Mom's house. Dad agreed that since we all wanted to be at the hospital anyway, it was easier on everyone if we came and went with Tom or Uncle Jacob. When the baby came home, Max and I would go back to Dad's condo—Max to stay, and me for the rest of the summer. I was surprised to realize I was a little disappointed. I didn't want to be away from the baby. Maybe I could visit on weekdays while Dad was at work.

Mom was up and around. In fact, they would have let her go home, but she insisted that as long as her baby was in the hospital, she'd be there all the time, anyway. Tom was willing to pay for the hospital room, so we all sort of camped out either there or in the waiting room outside the preemie nursery.

Mom called me into her hospital room one day to apologize. "I've talked to a doctor here, and I know I was wrong about Arien," she said simply. "Maybe I was just crazy with worry about the baby, but I wanted you to know I'm sorry, Cass. You were right to stick up for your friend."

I nodded dumbly, not knowing what else to say. I was glad Mom changed her mind, but what good would it do now? I couldn't even get in to see Arien.

We could see the baby, though. The nurses put Mom and Tom in sterile gowns, caps, and masks, and they went into the preemie nursery to hold the baby and feed her. Max, Nick, and I watched Mom gently rock the baby, careful not to disturb any of the wires, and every day Tom came out with a "weight report":

"She lost two ounces. But the nurse says that's normal."

"She gained an ounce."

"She gained three ounces."

"She had a little fever last night. She lost an ounce."

"The fever broke! She gained two ounces."

I still hadn't been to see Arien. Every morning, on my way to the nursery, I stopped at the information desk and asked if Arien Belle was allowed visitors. "No visitors," the pink lady would answer crisply. "Absolutely none."

When our baby was a week old (or twenty-nine weeks, as Max would be quick to point out), Tom came out to the nursery waiting room, all smiles. "She made it! She weighs five pounds, eight ounces! We're going home this afternoon!"

Max, Nick, and I jumped up and gave each other high fives, and Uncle Jacob snorted. "About time! Let's get this kid home so we can really fatten her up!"

Mom came out of the nursery, too, and pulled the surgical mask off her face. "So what are we going to name this kid?" she asked. Max, Nick, Tom, and Uncle Jacob all began to give their opinions, but I slipped away from the group and down the hall. If we were leaving the hospital, this might be my last chance. I didn't think they'd *ever* let anyone in to see Arien, and I simply had to try to find her.

I knew she was somewhere on the fifth floor, so I took the elevator, got off, and walked up to the bustling nurses' station. I held my head high and tried to act as if I knew exactly what I was doing.

"Arien Belle, please," I told a nurse. "I have a message for Mrs. Belle."

The nurse checked a list and pointed down the hall. "Room 515," she said. "Mrs. Belle will be inside the door."

When I pushed open the door to room 515, I saw that it was really a room that led to another room. In the first room there were a couple of chairs, a dozen machines, a stack of green hospital gowns, masks, and a box of plastic gloves. A bright red trash can in the room read, *Warning! Contaminated Materials!*

There was a large window that looked into the smaller room, where someone lay in a bed. Mrs. Belle was there, and there was this other person who looked like a spacewoman. It was a nurse, but she was wearing a helmet connected to some kind of strange backpack. She wore a long-sleeved suit, gloves, long pants, and even had plastic covers on her shoes.

I watched the eerie scene for a few minutes, then the nurse and Mrs. Belle turned to leave. As Mrs. Belle left the side of the bed, I could see Arien. She seemed thinner, but otherwise she hadn't changed.

The nurse was surprised to see me. "What are you doing here?" she snapped, after taking off her helmet. "You're not supposed to be here."

"It's OK," Mrs. Belle said, slipping into a chair. "Cassie is Arien's friend."

"I'd like to see her," I said, motioning toward the door. "Can I go in?"

"It's against hospital policy," the nurse snapped again. "We can't allow you to take the risk."

"Look at you!" Mrs. Belle said, turning in anger on the nurse. "Wearing that stupid contraption in there just so you won't breathe the same air she does! You won't touch her skin, you won't wipe her tears, and now you won't even let her see a friend." Mrs. Belle's voice became low and firm. "Don't let her die in loneliness. If her friend wants to go in, let her."

"I can't allow it," the nurse said. "But what you do is your business." The nurse turned sharply on her crepe-soled shoe and left the room.

Mrs. Belle nodded slightly, then looked at me. "She's missed you, Cassie," she said. "I know she'd love to see you. Go on in."

"I'm not afraid," I said, pausing. "But shouldn't I wear a mask or something? You know, to protect Arien?"

"No," Mrs. Belle answered. "Doctors say that is nothing but reverse discrimination these days. You really can't hurt her, and she can't hurt you. Cassie's doctor doesn't even wear gloves unless he's planning to give her a shot or something. That nurse's getup is crazy, but some people are still paranoid about this disease."

I nodded, still a little uncertain. "Is she OK?" I'd never had a friend in the hospital before.

"Her spirits are fine, but she's got pneumocystis carinii pneumonia," Mrs. Belle said. "The doctors call it PCP. It's pretty serious." She opened the door to Arien's room. "Thanks, Cassie."

I stepped inside.

"Arien? Are you asleep?"

She opened her eyes, and I thought they looked cloudier than usual. Otherwise, except for the IV in her arm and the tube running around her head under her nose, she seemed fine.

"Hi, Cassie," she said pleasantly, trying to smile. "I hear you have a new baby sister."

"I do. She's beautiful, Arien. You were right about her. It's going to be neat to have a baby at home."

She turned her head in my direction. "I'm glad you came. I wanted to thank you."

"For what?"

"For this." She reached for the bedstand to the left of the bed, and I noticed how bony her arm seemed. She really had lost a lot of weight. From a small drawer, she pulled out a folded piece of notebook paper.

She handed it to me, and I unfolded it. I recognized my handwriting instantly—it was the paper I had used to practice writing the last stanza of "Thanatopsis." I must have left it at the skating rink.

"So live, that when thy summons comes to join . . ." Arien whispered.

"You found this? You saved this?"

"Yes," she whispered. "And I love it. Especially that part about being soothed by an unfaltering trust. I'm trusting in God, Cassie, thanks to you."

187

I nodded. "You'll be OK, Arien."

She smiled, and a tear came into her eye. "I know. And best of all, I know I did something to stop this disease."

"You did?"

She nodded. "I didn't spread it to anyone else. My AIDS will stop with me. No one else will die because of me. I'm grateful for that."

I'd never thought of it that way. I never realized a person with AIDS could help stop the disease simply by not passing it to someone else.

"You'll be OK, Arien. As soon as you get over this pneumonia, you'll be training again. The nationals are coming up really soon, you know. What is it, two weeks?"

Arien nodded. "Two weeks."

"OK, then. So concentrate on getting over this and getting back to work. Remember that gold medal you wanted to bring Coach Davison?"

She smiled at me, and her eyes seemed to gently rebuke me. "I'm tired, Cass," she said quietly.

"No," I urged, waving my hands frantically. "On the day of victory, no one is tired, remember? When you win, you'll forget about all this. It'll be worth it."

"Sure, Cass," she said quietly.

Mrs. Belle rapped on the window and pointed to her watch. "You'd better go," Arien said. "The doctor's due to come in soon, and he'll have a fit if you're here when he comes."

I smiled extra-big, then leaned down and gave her a hug, careful not to disturb any of the machinery that surrounded her. "I'll see you soon, OK?"

"'Bye, Cass."

Two weeks later I sat at home in my best dress watching ESPN with Nick, Tom, Max, Uncle Jacob, and Mom. My tiny sister lay in my arms, drinking her bottle, and Mom was resting with her head on Tom's shoulder. It had been a long day, and the funeral had been rough. Everyone in my family went, and of course Mr. and Mrs. Belle were there. The absent ones were Coach Davison, Tommy, and Arien. Her body had been flown to California; she was going to be buried at home.

My mom had surprised me. She had hugged Mrs. Belle and murmured something about Arien's courage and friendship. She even let Mrs. Belle hold the baby—that amazed me—and when Mrs. Belle asked the baby's name, I saw them hug again.

The day wasn't over, though; there was still another chapter of Arien's life I had to close. Mrs. Belle said Arien wanted Coach and Tommy to go on to the nationals no matter what happened to her, and just before she died, she had whispered something about a victory lap. Mrs. Belle asked me what she meant, and I couldn't explain it. I wasn't exactly sure myself.

Now we were watching the national roller-skating championship competition in Lewisville, Texas, and Tommy McLaughlin was skating in the solo dance category to George Gershwin's "Rhapsody in Blue." A month ago, I would never have believed Tommy would compete, much less do as well as he was doing. But he skated with a flair and passion I'd never seen before.

At one point he did Arien's inverted camel spin, and Uncle Jacob whistled in appreciation. "That boy's great," he said, his unlit cigar bobbing up and down. "And you go to school with this kid, Cass?"

"Yep," I said proudly, putting the baby bottle more carefully into my sister's delicate rosebud mouth. "He was in my English class last year."

We all stayed in the den, quietly watching, until the winners were announced. I wasn't surprised at all that Tommy McLaughlin was announced as the gold-medal winner in the solo dance category. He stepped onto the center platform as the medal was hung around his neck, and the crowd in Texas stamped, cheered, and yelled. The crowd in our den broke into applause, too, and Nick whooped so loudly the baby started crying.

I jiggled her softly in my arms, trying to soothe her, and I saw Tommy take the medal from his neck and hold it high in the air. He moved his mouth as he triumphantly held the medal aloft, and I think I was probably the only person in the world who read his lips and knew that he said, "For Arien!"

"On the day of victory, no one is tired." I could see Arien saying it, even now, her blue-green eyes twinkling as she pushed herself to be the best. She wasn't tired now. She was having one forever-long day of victory.

"Come on, Stephanie Arien Harris," I said, taking the baby upstairs to her bassinet in Mom's room. "Would you like to hear a naptime story? Once upon a time, there was an amazing girl from California who was almost as pretty as you are. . . ."